NIGHT OF THE VAM-WOLF-ZOM

NIGHT OF THE VAM-WOLF-ZOM

BY
Steven Banks

ILLUSTRATED BY Mark Fearing

HOLIDAY HOUSE  New York

Text copyright © 2022 by Steven Banks

Illustrations copyright © 2022 by Mark Fearing

All Rights Reserved

HOLIDAY HOUSE is registered in the U.S. Patent and Trademark Office.

Printed and bound in April 2022 at Toppan Leefung, DongGuan City, China.

www.holidayhouse.com

First Edition

1 3 5 7 9 10 8 6 4 2

Library of Congress Cataloging-in-Publication Data

Names: Banks, Steven, 1954- author. | Fearing, Mark, illustrator.

Title: Night of the Vam-Wolf-Zom / by Steven Banks ; illustrated by Mark
Fearing.

Description: First edition. | New York : Holiday House, [2022] | Series:
Middle school bites ; #4 | Audience: Ages 8–12. | Audience: Grades 4–6.
Summary: "Eleven-year-old Tom the Vam-Wolf-Zom meets the zombie who
bit him, who is a pretty nice guy, but even the nicest monster can't
help Tom with middle school conundrums like band arguments, former
bullies, and his first kiss"— Provided by publisher.

Identifiers: LCCN 2021970003 | ISBN 9780823452170 (hardcover)

Subjects: CYAC: Middle schools—Fiction. | Schools—Fiction.
Vampires—Fiction. | Werewolves—Fiction. | Zombies—Fiction. | Humorous
stories. | LCGFT: Novels. | Humorous fiction.

Classification: LCC PZ7.B22637 Ni 2022 | DDC [Fic]—dc23

LC record available at https://lccn.loc.gov/2021970003

ISBN: 978-0-8234-5217-0 (hardcover)

To Sally Morgridge,
who said "Yes" after twenty book
publishing companies said "No."
If it wasn't for her, you wouldn't
be reading this.

Lesson: Don't give up.

1.

Conversations with a Zombie

I wish I hadn't been turned into a Vam-Wolf-Zom. Then I wouldn't be talking to a zombie and worried that a vampire was going to kill me for ditching her instead of fighting a werewolf.

I wish I was just a regular kid going to middle school. I wish my biggest problem was a math test I hadn't studied for, or wondering if someone liked me, or forgetting to read three chapters of *Bridge to Terabithia*, or not being able to open my locker.

But I'm a Vam-Wolf-Zom. The only one in the world.

Three Reasons It Had Been a Very Bad Day

- I'd saved the life of the worst person at Hamilton Middle School: Tanner Gantt.
- Darcourt, the werewolf who turned *me* into a werewolf, had stolen the book *A Vampiric Education*, which was worth a million dollars and full of vampire secrets.
- Martha Livingston, the vampire who bit me, had lent me the book and was going to kill me for losing it.

Martha and I had turned into bats to chase Darcourt on his motorcycle. But then I saw a carnival trailer below us, and inside it was the zombie who had bitten me. It might be my one and only chance to ever talk to him.

I landed on top of the zombie's trailer, turned into smoke—a vampire trick I had finally learned—and slipped inside through a crack in the door. He was your typical zombie. Gray skin, stringy hair, some scars on his face and white eyes. I always imagined zombies smelled really bad, like rotting flesh. He didn't, which was a big relief because of my werewolf sense of smell. Ever since I turned into a Vam-Wolf-Zom, I'd been discovering that a lot of things weren't what I'd thought they'd be.

The zombie said, "Hullo."

I *think* he said "hullo." That's what it sounded like. It was kind of noisy in the moving trailer. It might have just been a grunt. Do zombies talk? Sometimes they talked in the movies. I hoped he could talk. I wanted to ask him some questions.

The zombie opened his mouth again. Was he trying to bite me? Do zombies eat other zombies?

"Hullo," he said again.

"You can talk?" I asked.

He answered in a deep, croaky voice. "Reckon I just did." He sounded like the cowboy actor guy with the big droopy moustache in those western movies my dad watches. "My name's Dusty."

"I'm Tom."

"Pleased to make your acquaintance."

"Do you remember biting me about four months ago?"

"Well now, truth be told, I didn't bite you."

"What are you talking about? You bit me! That's why I'm part zombie!"

"Nope. I was tryin' to scare you away by openin' my mouth, *pretendin'* to bite you. Figured you were the skittish type. You put your hands up in front of your face and your palm went and hit my top teeth."

Technically that was true. That sort of made me mad. I hate it when stuff is my fault.

"So, you didn't want to eat me?" I asked.

"Son, I haven't partook of humans for, let me see now, been ten years."

"I don't eat people either," I told him.

"Trust me, they don't taste as good as they look."

"So, what do you eat?"

"Whatever Boss Man brings me. Pizza, cheese-burgers, and corn dogs mostly."

My best friend, Zeke, would love that diet.

"When'd you become a zombie?" I asked.

"'Bout fifteen years ago near as I can recollect. My mind gets a little fuzzy nowadays."

"What were you before you were a zombie?"

He sighed. "A human being."

"No, I meant what did you do?"

"I was a brain surgeon."

"Really?!"

"Yep. I used to fix brains . . . and then, I ate 'em."
He smiled. "That's a joke, son. I was a bull rider in
rodeos. Folks called me Dusty on account I fell off a
lot more than I stayed on."

The trailer changed lanes and went around a
curve, so I wobbled a bit.

"Whyn't you set yourself down on that box,"
said Dusty.

I sat down on a wooden box that had DR.
NUT written on the side. "Who turned you into a
zombie?"

"That's a good story."

2.

A Good Story

She was a little squirt of a gal. Dark hair, brown eyes, and very sharp teeth. I was out at the corral, late at night, and she came up to me. I thought she was a fan. Then, she went and bit me. That's how life is, full of surprises. One day you're ridin' bulls, next day you wanna take a big ol' bite out of 'em."

"How'd you end up in a carnival?"

"Long version or short version?"

"Better do the short one, I can't stay very long." I needed to get back to Martha to help her get the vampire book from Darcourt.

"Back in my people eatin' days, I was wanderin' around the woods lookin' for somethin' to eat. I saw a carnival that was settin' up in a big field. They had a poster of a big ol' snake on the side of a trailer. I went inside and there was my dinner: a six-foot long python in a glass case. I moseyed on up, lifted the lid, and ate it. Python was surprised. He thought he was gonna eat *me*. Then, Boss Man came in and got mighty upset that I'd eaten the star of his show. But quick as can be, he figured I'd make a purty good replacement. He moved faster than a jackrabbit. Threw a blanket over me, and roped and hog-tied me before I could skedaddle on out of there and escape. Been here ever since."

"Does anyone else know you're a real zombie?"

"Nope. Just Boss Man. Everybody else thinks I'm a dummy or a feller wearin' a mask. I sit here in this chair every day. People stare. I growl. Pretend I'm gonna eat 'em. They scream and run out. And that's basically my life." Dusty sighed and looked sort of sad.

Life is weird. The first time I saw him, I was afraid of him. Then he bit me and turned me into a zombie, so I was mad at him. Now, I felt sorry for him, tied up to a chair in an old, dirty trailer.

"It's nice to talk to a fellow walker. It's been a while," he said. Then he leaned forward, as much as he could, and looked at my face. "Hope you don't mind me askin', but you look like you got some other stuff goin' on too."

I explained I was a Vam-Wolf-Zom, and told him how it all happened. He let out a long, low whistle and shook his head.

"Well now, that is one big piece of bad luck. Can't say I ever met one of them before."

"I'm the only one in the world, I think."

"Your trail must be mighty rough at times."

"Yeah. It is."

Nobody ever asks me if it's hard being a Vam-Wolf-Zom. Dusty was a lot nicer than the other two people who bit me. Martha Livingston got mad really easily. Darcourt acted nice and friendly at first, but he was faking it. Just like Tanner Gantt when I met him in second grade. I wish there was an app on your phone that could tell you who was actually nice and who was just pretending.

The truck pulling the trailer started to slow down.

"Must be gettin' near our next stop," said Dusty. "Or Boss Man's gotta eat."

I peeked through the crack under the door. The truck was pulling off the highway into a Burger Barn parking lot. My stomach and Dusty's growled at the same time.

We came to a stop. I heard the truck door open, and then slam shut, and footsteps walking away.

"I bet Boss Man'd love to put you on exhibit," said Dusty. "You'd be a star attraction, bring in some of them big bucks. You prob'ly shouldn't be hangin' around here too long."

"Good point." I had one more question I wanted to ask him. "Hey. I went back to the gas station where you bit me—"

"Tried to *scare* you," he corrected me.

"Right. It had burned down, but your trailer was still there. I saw footprints leaving the trailer."

"I tried to escape and Boss Man caught me. Zombie's ain't exactly known for their speed."

"Some zombies in movies can run really fast."

"Well, movies and TV shows and books ain't the same as real life. Important thing to remember."

"Where were you trying to go?"

"You ever heard of . . . Zombie Nirvana?"

"No. Is that a movie?"

"Sounds like one, don't it? No, it's a place I heard tell of once. A fellow walker told me 'bout it." Dusty shrugged. "Might be real. Might be one of them old wive's tales."

"What is it exactly?"

"S'posed to be a place where they let zombies live in a contained area. The sign says 'Zombie Nirvana. Zombies Roam Wild and Free.' They feed 'em and just let 'em be. Run by somebody who's partial to zombies for some reason."

"I've never heard of a place like that," I said.

"Well, I'm guessin' they don't want people sniffin' around. Folks might get upset if they knew there was a mess o' walkers somewhere. But . . . if it was a real place and I could get there, I'd be one happy and contented cowboy."

"Where is it?"

"S'posed to be 'round these parts. Feller gave me a map a ways back."

He reached in his pants pocket, which wasn't too easy to do since he was tied up, and pulled out an old, crumpled-up piece of paper. I took it and unfolded it. It was an old restaurant placemat from some place called Bubba's Big-Time Barbecue.

Barbecued meat sounded really good right now. I was getting hungry. On the back was a hand-drawn map in pencil, with scribbled directions and arrows. ROUTE 66 to HIGHWAY 61 to OLD MILL ROAD, leading to a big circle with ZOMBIE NIRVANA written in the middle and a big *X*.

I handed the map back to Dusty and he said, "Carnival's only gonna be 'round here a few more weeks, and then we head out west. Boss Man wants to set up in a permanent location, some sorta museum of oddities. So, time is a-tickin'. This may be my last chance."

"I wish I was old enough to drive," I said. "I'd take you there."

BAM! BAM! BAM!

Somebody was pounding on the trailer door.

3.

Dinner Is Served

Wake up! Chow time!" yelled a man with a high voice from outside the trailer.

"That's Boss Man," said Dusty. "You'd better hide."

I quickly whispered, "Turn to bat, bat I shall be!" and flew behind a wooden bowl on the floor. A short, skinny man with long hair and tattoos, wearing a T-shirt that said, EDDIE VAN HALEN LIVES!, unlocked the door and came in. He was holding a paper bag. He reached inside and pulled out five little-kid-sized hamburgers. Burger Barn calls them Baby Burgers, though I don't think many babies actually eat them. They smelled delicious.

I have to admit, I prefer Baby Burgers. They taste better for some reason even though they have the same exact stuff on them as the regular burgers. But if you order Baby Burgers people make fun of you. So, you end up eating something you don't like as much because you don't want to be embarrassed. I wish I didn't get embarrassed at all. I could do whatever I wanted, and wouldn't care if people laughed. Like Zeke. He always orders Baby Burgers.

Dusty was right. if Boss Man knew there was a Vam-Wolf-Zom hiding in the corner, he'd try to lock me up so fast. When I first turned into a Vam-Wolf-Zom, my sister, Emma, wanted to sell me to a circus so she could buy a car. She was not kidding. My parents didn't let her do it.

"Dinner is served!" said Boss Man.

He stood there and threw the baby burgers at Dusty, who had to catch them in his mouth and eat without using his hands. Boss Man threw them really fast and hard, like he was throwing baseballs.

"Here's the wind up and the pitch! That's a fastball! Right in the pie hole! Don't forget to chew before you swallow. Mmmm! Don't that taste good?"

Sometimes Dusty didn't catch them and they fell on the floor.

"Oops! You missed that one! Back to the minors!"

After a while he got tired of throwing burgers and he reached down for the bowl I was hiding behind. I rolled myself up into a tiny bat ball and he didn't see me. Boss Man put the rest of the burgers in the bowl and set it on a tray that was attached to a long stick, so he didn't have to get too close to Dusty. Dusty leaned down and gobbled up the burgers from the bowl. It was like watching a starving dog eat.

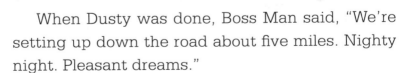

When Dusty was done, Boss Man said, "We're setting up down the road about five miles. Nighty night. Pleasant dreams."

He went out of the trailer, closed the door behind him, and locked it. I changed back into me.

"Pardon my table manners," said Dusty. "Ain't so easy eatin' without the use of your hands."

"That's okay."

"There're a coupla burgers on the ground, if you don't mind a bit of dirt."

"Uh, no thanks, I'll get something later."

I picked up the two burgers and gave them to Dusty. I didn't want to leave him, but I had to. Martha Livingston was probably getting madder every second I stayed.

"Dusty, I gotta get going. I need to help my friend."

"Helpin' a friend is one of the best things you can do in life. Thanks for droppin' by. Pleasure to meet you, Tom. Sorry I accidentally brought you into the zombie world, but . . . unfortunate things happen, don't they? Maybe our paths'll cross again down the road a-piece."

"Yeah . . . maybe."

"Happy trails."

I changed to smoke and went out through the crack. Outside, I turned into a bat and flew away. I had to find Martha and Darcourt as fast as I could.

I flew back to the place over the highway where Martha had yelled at me. I decided to keep flying in the direction we'd been going. I sniffed to see if I could catch Darcourt's scent, which I did after about ten minutes. I tracked the smell going off the highway and down a dirt road that had motorcycle tire tracks. Since I was in the woods, I kept an eye out for owls or hawks that might want to eat me for dinner. I followed the tire tracks until I saw something I wished I hadn't seen.

4.

Aftermath

Darcourt's motorcycle had crashed into a tree. The front wheel was bent, and a few feet away there was some of Darcourt's fur on the ground, streaked with blood. Then, I saw something that made my stomach turn. A small, torn piece of Martha's dress—with *claw marks* on it.

I bent down and sniffed the blood. Werewolf. I looked around and saw a torn page from *A Vampiric Education*. It was the page signed by Lovick Zabrecky, the vampire who had turned Martha in

1776. He had written that if she lost the book or gave it away, he would hunt her down. *"When I find you, it will be an unpleasant experience."*

I sniffed the air. Darcourt's scent was all mixed up with other animals in the woods, so I couldn't track him. I started to feel bad that I had abandoned Martha to talk to Dusty. But it wasn't totally my fault that Darcourt had the book. Martha shouldn't have lent it to me. And if she hadn't bitten me, I wouldn't be a vampire in the first place! But I still felt bad.

"Martha!" I yelled into the darkness.

No answer.

"Martha!" I yelled louder.

Nothing.

I flew around using my night vision to look for her until I heard an owl hoot. It was getting late, and I had to get out of there. As I flew home, I wondered what might have happened.

Who won the fight? Where were they now? Who had the book? If Darcourt had it, would he give it to the Council of Werewolves, or the group Martha said was worse, the Society of Shape-Shifters? Would Darcourt come back if he didn't have the book? How mad was Martha?

Darcourt was big and strong, but Martha was super smart and could turn into a bat, or smoke, and maybe even hypnotize him. She was also 244 years old and had probably fought a lot of werewolves. I bet she'd outsmarted him and gotten the book back somehow. If she hadn't, I hoped she wasn't waiting at my house.

o o o

When I got home Martha wasn't there, which was a relief, but Emma was, which was almost worse. She barged into my room without knocking, like she always does.

"What happened to you?" she demanded. "You ran off after that Darcourt guy and left us at Comic-Con. We looked for you for, like, forever!"

I seriously doubted that.

"Uh, I had to do some Vam-Wolf-Zom stuff."

"Where'd Darcourt go?"

I knew she didn't really care about me. Emma was in love with Darcourt. She can fall in love with people in, like, five minutes. If she knew he was a werewolf she wouldn't be in love with him. Or maybe she would? Girls loved werewolves in movies. But like Dusty said, "Movies ain't the same as real life."

"Did he say anything about me?" she asked. "Do you think he likes me? Do you have his phone number?"

"I thought you had a boyfriend, Emma?"

"I do! But . . . I can just be friends with a guy."

"No way! Not a tall handsome one that you're in love with."

"That's not true! You . . . you are so immature!"

She made her growly noise, turned around, and slammed the door.

"Whoever slammed that door owes me a dollar!" yelled Dad from the living room. He'd started a new "No Door Slamming" rule and there was a $1.00 fine for each slam.

"It wasn't me!" yelled Emma.

"Yes, it was!" I yelled.

"I know it was you, Emma!" yelled Dad. "I recognize your slam!"

"That's impossible!" yelled Emma.

"Stop yelling!" yelled Mom.

∘ ∘ ∘

After thinking about it, I decided not to tell Zeke about Dusty and Zombie Nirvana. He has trouble keeping secrets. And I didn't want to have to hypnotize him again. I did that once to make him stop doing jumping jacks, but then I ended up missing him doing them.

I checked the website Martha told me about, the one that alerted her when Darcourt was in the area. The site read: THIS WEBSITE IS NO LONGER AVAILABLE. My phone buzzed. It was a text from Martha. I took a deep breath and read it.

I fought Darcourt and vanquished him. I have the book.

I felt better. Then I read the rest of the text.

We shall never speak or meet again.

Martha Livingston.

5.

The Invitation

The next morning, I almost missed the school bus. I forgot to put on my sunscreen and had to run back home. When I got on the bus, Annie was reading a book, Capri was drawing a picture of a heart in the sky, Dog Hots was asleep, and Zeke was squishing his nose against the window. I sat down next to Annie.

"Hey, Annie, what're you reading?"

She held up the book. "*True Grit*. It's about this fourteen-year-old girl who hires a cowboy to help her avenge her father. It's really good."

That made me think of Dusty.

Annie looked up. "Nesmith approaching . . ."

Maren Nesmith was coming down the aisle toward us and had a big fake smile. She probably wanted to tell us about a fancy place she went to or some expensive thing her parents bought her.

"Hey, guys! Do you still have your band, Conjunction?"

Annie rolled her eyes. "Our name is Conundrum."

"Triple awesome! And you're still in it, Tom?"

"Yeah," I said. Why'd she ask that?

"Triple awesome! My birthday is in, like, two weeks."

Maren had *never* invited any of us to one of her birthday parties.

"Are you inviting us to your party?" asked Capri.

"No—I mean yes! I want your band to play. It's on Saturday night, the twentieth, and it's going to be triple awesome!"

"Triple awesome" was her new favorite expression. It was triple annoying.

"We're going to have ten kinds of pizza! And a caricature artist! And a magician! And a DJ! And a dance floor! And a doughnut tree!"

"A doughnut tree?!" said Zeke. "Excellent! What time?"

"Six o'clock."

Dog Hots had woken up. "How much are you paying us?" he asked. He didn't like Maren either, but he liked money.

"I have to pay you?" she said, making a face.

"Yeah," said Annie. "We don't play for free unless it's a benefit for a worthy cause, like rescue animals or saving nature."

"No prob! I'll call my mom on my new It-Phone 20!" She whipped out her red phone and waved it in our faces. "Have you guys seen it?"

"Yes," I said. "You've shown it to us a million times."

"It's triple awesome! Be right back!"

She walked down the aisle to where she always sits. When I knew she wouldn't hear me I said, "I don't want to play at her party! Maren is a total jerk!"

Nobody was going to argue with me about that. The first day I told the school I was a Vam-Wolf-Zom, Maren thought I was going to bite her and suck her blood. She moved to a desk far away from me in English. She always kept about ten feet between us when I saw her in the hall.

"But I wanna do it!" said Zeke. "She told us she's got a ginormous pool!"

"It's February, Zeke," I said. "Nobody's going to go swimming."

"I'll bring my wet suit," he said.

"You don't have a wet suit."

"I can make one out of my rubber raincoat and duct tape."

Zeke thinks you can make anything with duct tape.

"I would like see her wiener doodle dog," said Capri. Maren was always bragging about that dog. Its name was Precious, which made me want to throw up.

"It'll probably bite you," I said.

"I'd like to check out her house," said Dog Hots. He doesn't like Maren either, but besides liking money, he has a crush on her. I don't know how that is possible. How can you have a crush on somebody you don't like?

"Why isn't she hiring 5ive Cute Boys to play?" I said. They were a famous band with a song called "I Love Your Face." Maren loved them.

"Her parents are rich, but they're not *that* rich," said Annie.

Maren wasn't a jerk because she was rich. Shay Barndell was really nice, and she was rich, and Otto Fite was way richer than Maren or Shay, and he was nice too. Maren was just a jerk.

"Well, I can't do it that night," I said. I needed a good excuse. "I have to go to my sister's harp recital."

"You said Emma quit playing harp," said Zeke.

Why does Zeke remember every single thing I tell him?

"She's baaacck," whispered Dog Hots.

Maren was coming down the aisle toward us.

"Okay! It's all set."

"How much are you paying us?" asked Dog Hots.

She told us.

"Each?" said a surprised Annie. It was a lot of money. Nobody thought we'd get that much.

"Yeah."

Annie pretended to be thinking. "We'll have to ask Abel."

"Let me know by lunch time," said Maren, and she went back to her friends.

Everybody looked at me.

I pretended to play with the zipper on my backpack. "Well . . . Maybe I can miss Emma's harp recital. And I guess we could do it for the practice."

I have to admit it, I like money too.

"Okay," said Annie. "Tom, ask Abel if he can do it."

o o o

Abel was at our locker, wearing a dark blue striped suit, writing his daily quote on the dry-erase board he'd hung up.

"ALWAYS HAVE A WILLING HAND TO HELP SOMEONE, YOU MIGHT BE THE ONLY ONE THAT DOES." —ROY T. BENNETT

That made me think of Dusty.

"Good morning, Mr. Marks," said Abel. "Hope your weekend was pleasant."

It wasn't but I said it was. "You're not going to believe this, but Maren Nesmith asked us to play at her birthday party a week from Saturday. She's gonna pay us. You wanna do it?"

Abel put away the dry-erase pen. "Interesting... Do you think she has an ulterior motive of some sort?"

"What do you mean?"

"A concealed or secret reason for asking us, beyond wanting us to play."

"Maybe . . . I don't know."

He grabbed a book and put it in his briefcase. "An engagement of this sort would be quite beneficial to our collective experience as musicians."

So, everybody in the band had a reason to do it.

"Hey, Abel, have you ever heard of a place called Zombie Nirvana?"

He closed his eyes for about five seconds, then opened them. "No. I can't say that I have. An intriguing name. May I inquire why you are interested?"

"Uh, nothing. Just heard the name."

Abel knew everything. If he hadn't heard of Zombie Nirvana, it probably didn't exist. It was a good thing that Dusty didn't try to go there and get disappointed. That made me feel a little better. But if it was a secret place, how would Abel know about it? And there was that map. That made me feel bad again.

6.

Are You Really Tanner Gantt?

Hey, Marks."

The voice behind me sounded like Tanner Gantt, but he never called me Marks, or Tom. It was always Freaky or Creepy or something mean. I turned around. It *was* him. He was peeking out from under the stairway to the second floor. He looked nervous, like he was about to get in trouble.

"Come here," he said.

I walked over.

He lowered his voice. "Did you tell anyone what happened yesterday?"

He meant when I saw him getting beat up by Dennis Hannigan and he was crying like a baby, and I saved his life.

"No."

That was true. I hadn't. But I *really* wanted to tell Zeke. And Annie and Abel and Capri and Dog Hots and basically the whole school.

"Are you gonna?" he asked.

I closed my eyes, like Abel did, and pretended to think. Then, I opened them. "I don't know . . ."

I'd made Hannigan promise to never do anything to Tanner Gantt or I'd suck his blood and eat his brain. I'd never do that, but Hannigan didn't know for sure.

Tanner Gantt looked around to make sure no one was listening.

"If you don't tell anybody what happened, I won't call you names anymore."

Would he really? You couldn't trust him. Should I get him to sign a legal document?

"Okay," I said.

"Okay," he said.

"*And* you can't make fun of any of my friends or do anything to them either."

He let out a big sigh. "Okay."

He started to walk away and then he stopped and turned around.

"Hey. Do you still have that band with Annie Barstow?"

"Yeah."

"You don't have a bass player, do you?"

"No."

He stood there for a second, like he was waiting for me to say something.

"Why?" I asked.

"Nothing," he said, and walked away.

o o o

"*What* is wrong with Tanner Gantt?" said Annie when we were all having lunch at our table in the cafeteria. "He walked by me and didn't say anything mean."

"Me too!" said Dog Hots. "I dropped a book, and he didn't laugh or kick it down the hall. He just walked by."

Capri said, "I bumped into him, and he actually said sorry."

Zeke turned to me. "Did you hypnotize him, T-Man?"

"No."

"Maybe somebody took out his brain and switched it for someone else's?" said Zeke.

Abel put down the banana bread pudding

he'd made and said, "Perhaps Mr. Gantt had an epiphany or traumatic experience which caused him to reevaluate his behavior and radically change his personality?" Did Abel know what happened? "One day's behavior does not mean a permanent change. However, he may be making a conscious effort to alter his innate nature in order to live a more satisfactory life."

"Or maybe Tanner Gantt's being nice because . . . we're in an alternate universe!" said Zeke.

I couldn't tell them why he was being nice because I'd have to tell them what happened. It was a conundrum.

7.

The Tanner Gantt Question

Tanner Gantt kept his word. He didn't call any of us names, and he didn't make fun of us or do anything bad. You could tell he was tempted sometimes, but he didn't. He even started saying "Hey" to me when I passed him in the hall. Zeke still thought his brain had been switched or we were in another dimension.

We were eating lunch in the cafeteria a few days later when I looked up from my double cheeseburger and quietly said, "You guys . . . don't look . . . but Tanner Gantt's coming over here."

They all looked! Why do people always do that? He walked toward our table and everybody tensed up. It was a natural reaction. We'd been doing that for seven years.

"Hey," he said.

Did he want to have lunch with us? That had never happened in the history of the world.

"What do you want?" asked Annie cautiously.

"I heard your band is gonna play at Maren's party."

Did Maren invite him to her party? No one ever invited him to their parties. The last party I saw him at was Mason Cameron's in first grade. He made her cry, poured punch on Esteban Marquez, pushed a kid named Connor into a wading pool, and stole one of the gifts.

"Yeah. Our band's playing," said Annie.

"Why don't you have a bass player?" he asked.

"'Cause we don't," said Dog Hots.

"You'd sound a lot better if you did."

"Why do you care?" asked Annie.

"I thought, maybe, um, I could play bass with you."

Zeke almost fainted. Capri dropped her tofu burger. Abel spilled some tea on his gray suit jacket.

"Aren't you in that band, Skull Nightmare, with those eighth graders?" I asked.

"We broke up. Nathanson sold his drums and Ross is moving to Arizona."

"Why do you want to play with us?" asked Annie.

He shrugged. "You don't suck. And nobody else at school has a band."

"We'll think about it," said Annie.

I couldn't believe she said that. Had Annie's brain been switched? I knew he was only being nice to us was because I'd saved his life. But being in our band? That was crazy.

○ ○ ○

"We are *not* having Tanner Gantt in our band!" I said after Tanner walked away.

"I agree!" said Zeke. "I'd rather have Bungee Badfinger in our band than him!"

Bungee Badfinger was the villain in the new *Rabbit Attacks* video game.

"I wouldn't be in a band with him for a million dollars!" said Dog Hots. He was totally lying, of course. He would be in a band with Voldemort, Darth Vader, the Wicked Witch of the West, and Thanos for a thousand bucks.

"I know," said Annie. "But . . . we do need a bass player."

"His personality has undergone a radical change for several days now," said Abel.

Capri shook her head. "'Once a bully, always a bully.' That's what my sobo says."

"Yeah, but people can change sometimes," said Annie.

"No, they can't!" I said. "They say they will, but they don't."

"You changed into a Vam-Wolf-Zom," said Zeke.

"That's one hundred percent different," I argued.

Annie said, "Remember the talent show? He's a really good bass player."

Abel nodded. "Musically speaking, we could use the addition of a solid sonic bottom end that a bass guitar provides."

Capri said, "That's true."

"Pretty much every band has a bass player," said Dog Hots.

I had to stop this from happening.

"Whoa! Wait! Time out! Are you guys forgetting all the things Tanner Gannt has done?!"

I had a list in my head.

Horrible Things Tanner Gantt Has Done

- Stole Zeke's skateboard.
- Broke Dog Hots's Peppa Pig pencil in 2nd grade.
- Put gum in Capri's hair. Twice.
- Threw Annie's *Beezus and Ramona* book on the roof in 1st grade.
- Called us a zillion different mean names.
- Made fun of Abel's suits and briefcase.
- Put garlic in my costume at the winter holiday show.
- Dressed up like a Vam-Wolf-Zom for Halloween.
- Stole my Vacuum Girl action figure and tried to sell it on eBay.
- Made a Vam-Wolf-Zom snowman.

I was about to start going down the list, but

Annie looked determined. She pushed her glasses up her nose with her finger.

"Here's how we do it: We try him out at practice on Wednesday. If he does *anything* we don't like, he's not in the band."

"But what if it's all a big trick?" said Zeke, nervously. "What if he does something really, really, really bad?"

"We don't have to worry," said Annie, looking over at me and smiling. "We have a Vam-Wolf-Zom to protect us."

I liked that Annie thought of me as a protector. I'd much rather protect her from Tanner Gant than protect him from Dennis Hannigan.

◦ ◦ ◦

In the hallway, between sixth and seventh period, Annie and I told Tanner Gannt he could try out for the band.

He got mad. "*What?* I have to try out? I play as good as you or Abel."

"Do you want to try out or not?" asked Annie.

Tanner Gantt crossed his big arms and then he uncrossed them. "Yeah . . . okay. When?"

"My house. Four o'clock tomorrow. And don't be late."

8.

Audition

Tanner Gantt showed up at 4:15 for band practice.

"You're late," said Annie, glaring at him when she opened the door.

"My mom's car wouldn't start."

He had his bass guitar slung over his shoulder. He didn't have a case for it. Next to him was a little kid's red wagon with his amplifier inside.

"You pulled your amp all the way over here in that wagon?" she asked.

"Yeah."

If he'd seen one of us using a toy wagon, he would have made fun of us for years.

He came inside with his stuff. His amplifier looked like a piece of junk.

"How come your amp is so beat up?" I asked. "Does it sound good?"

Abel said, "If I am not mistaken, that is a vintage Fender Bassman amplifier, circa 1971. Valued by many famous bass players for its exquisite sound."

Tanner Gantt said, "How'd you know that?"

"Abel knows everything," said Dog Hots.

"How did you acquire it?" asked Abel.

I bet he stole it.

"It was my dad's," he said.

Annie showed him where to plug in the amp and warned him, "If you're late again you're out of the band."

He turned on his amp. "I thought I wasn't in the band yet."

"Oh . . . yeah," she said. "Right."

Zeke was in the corner of Annie's living room, as far away from Tanner Gantt as possible, holding his banjo.

"Zeke, why are you in the corner?" I whispered.

"He's gonna do something," he nervously whispered back.

"Like what?"

"I don't know. But I wanna be far away when he does it."

Annie strapped on her guitar. "Okay, we'll play

a song for you, all the way through. Then I'll teach it to you, and you can try and play it with us."

Tanner Gantt shrugged.

"This song is called 'Plastic or Paper.' It's in the key of D."

We started playing. Tanner Gannt stared at Annie's hands on her guitar. We did two verses and the chorus, and then he started playing along with us. Annie gave him a dirty look. He was supposed to wait, but he had already figured out how to play it.

Perfectly.

As soon as he started playing, we sounded a million times better. We finally sounded like a real band. We gave each other quick looks, trying not to let Tanner Gantt see. Abel smiled and nodded to the beat. Dog Hots dropped a drumstick. Capri stopped playing piano until Annie nudged her with the top of her guitar and she started playing again.

Tanner Gannt was so good it made me kind of mad. I wish he'd been bad, so we wouldn't have to even think about letting him in. When we finished the song, nobody said anything.

"What's the matter?" he asked.

"Uh . . . nothing," said Annie.

"You want to do it again? I can sing on the chorus and harmonize, if you want?" he said.

"You can sing?" asked Annie.

"A little."

I'd heard Tanner Gantt sing once before. He was sitting on the swings in the park at night, all by himself, which is something he did a lot. He was an okay singer, I guess.

"We don't need you to sing," I said. "We already have two singers, me and Annie, and I harmonize with her on the chorus."

"I can sing the third part," he said.

"Three-part harmony would sound awesome," said Annie.

"But we only have two microphones," I argued.

"He can share with me," said Annie.

We did the song again. Tanner Gantt stood

on the other side of Annie's microphone. He leaned in close to sing during the chorus. But that wasn't the worst part.

It sounded amazing.

He was almost as good a singer as me.

After we finished the song, Annie said, "We need to have a private band meeting."

We all went in the kitchen and left Tanner Gannt in the living room.

"Somebody should stay in there and watch him, so he doesn't steal anything," said Zeke.

"You want to go in and stand guard?" asked Annie, sarcastically.

"No way!" said Zeke. "I'm not staying in there alone with him."

We formed a circle and talked quietly, so he wouldn't hear us, though he was probably trying to.

"Well? What do you guys think?" began Annie.

"He is a superb musician and singer," said Abel.

"You really think his singing's that good?" I asked.

"Indubitably," said Abel.

"We sound so much better!" said Capri.

"If he's in the band we could make millions!" said Dog Hots.

"You think so?" wondered Zeke.

"What do you think, Tom?" asked Annie.

"Um . . . I don't know . . . I guess he plays and sings okay."

Annie looked at me like I was crazy. "He plays and sings great." She frowned. "But I still haven't made up my mind."

∘ ∘ ∘

We all went back in the living room. Tanner Gantt was looking at pictures of Annie and her family on the wall. He turned around.

"So? Am I in or not?" he asked.

"I have a question first," said Annie. "You've been a total bully to us for years. What happened?"

He glanced over at me for a second, then looked back at Annie.

"Well . . . I just . . . decided to, you know, act different."

"Okay," she said. "We'll try you out at Maren's party. But if you do anything we don't like, you're out. Next practice is on Friday. Don't be late again."

o o o

The next day at school, things kept reminding me of Dusty. It was like the teachers got together and said, *Let's make Tom think about Dusty, so he helps him escape to Zombie Nirvana!*

In English, Mr. Kessler read us a short story called "The Lonesome Cowboy." In history, Mrs. Troller talked about World War II soldiers escaping from a prisoner camp. In art, Mr. Baker had put up a new poster that said DO THE RIGHT THING! And Mr. Stockdale had us sing a song called "Count On Me" in choir.

I know how bad it is to be a zombie, but it had to be even worse to be tied to a chair, locked up in a dark, dirty, old trailer all the time. Having people stare at you. And having Boss Man throw food at you.

On the bus ride home, I decided I had to try and get Dusty to Zombie Nirvana. But I couldn't do it by myself. And I realized there was only one person who could help me.

9.

Hatching the Plan

This is Luc-Bot to Em-Bot! Do you read me?"

"Affirmative, Luc-Bot! Em-Bot reads you loud and clear!"

Emma and her boyfriend, Carrot Boy, had the stupidest new nicknames: Em-Bot and Luc-Bot. They got them from the Second Most Boring Movie Ever, about two robots who fall in love, called *Romeo-Droid and Juliet-Cyborg.* Emma was forcing Carrot Boy to watch it. He wanted to watch *Escape from Planet of the Pimple People,* which is a million times better. But Emma always wins.

If their nicknames weren't bad enough, they'd also decided to speak in robot voices. It was totally annoying.

"Does Luc-Bot need energy boost?"

"Negative, Em-Bot. Luc-Bot systems fully charged."

I wanted to terminate both of them.

They were lying on the sofa wrapped up like a pretzel. It looked uncomfortable, but they didn't seem to mind. Because the movie was so boring, Carrot Boy kept falling asleep and Emma kept jabbing him awake with her elbow.

"Why has Luc-Bot shut down?"

Carrot Boy opened his eyes. "Negative, Em-Bot. Have not shut down."

"Luc-Bot's eyes were closed! Missing best part of movie!"

There were no "best parts" in that movie.

"Uh . . . Luc-Bot not sleeping. Closing eyes to save energy and let words wash over me."

"That does not compute, Luc-Bot!"

I wasn't paying much attention to them because I was making a list in my head.

Six Reasons Carrot Boy Could Help Me Save Dusty

- He had a car.
- He loved carnivals.
- He loved zombies.
- He loved movies about people escaping from places.
- If he could help a nice zombie get to a zombie refuge, he probably would.
- He was a good person, even though he liked Emma for some strange reason.

I pretended to watch the movie for a while and then I hatched my plan. I had to remind myself to call him by his real name. Carrot Boy was what Emma used to call him because of his red hair, before he became her boyfriend.

"Hey, Lucas, do you like carnivals?"

"I love carnivals!"

"There's an awesome carnival up near Clarksville. You want to go?"

"Dude, that's pretty far away. It's like a two-hour drive."

He wasn't doing his robot voice and Emma got mad.

"Luc-Bot! You are a robot!"

He started doing it again.

"Sorry, Em-Bot! Forgot! System failure! Tom-Bot, that is two-hour drive."

I said, "Yeah, I know, but it's rated five stars on the Best Carnival Rating Site." (I made that up. There's no such site.) "You wanna drive me there next weekend? I'll pay for your ticket."

"Affirmative, Tom-Bot! Em-Bot, prepare for expedition to carnival!"

Emma stopped doing her annoying robot voice and did her normal annoying voice.

"No! Way! Carnivals are gross! The rides are dangerous and the people that work there are creepy-scary!"

I let Emma rant for a while.

"The food is all salty, sugary, greasy, and deep fried, and the games are rigged so you don't win anything."

It was perfect. She'd never go with us. Maren's party was Friday, so we had to go rescue Dusty on Saturday.

"You don't have to come, Emma," I said. "Wanna go this Saturday, Lucas?"

"He can't," said Emma.

"Why not?" asked Carrot Boy.

"You've got to take me to my Irish step-dancing class."

She'd just started doing that. I knew she'd quit in a week, like everything else.

Carrot Boy sighed. "Oh . . . right. Sorry, dude."

I was not giving up. "What about Sunday?" That was the last day the carnival was open—my last chance to rescue Dusty.

"Are we doing anything Sunday, Emma?" he asked.

I could tell she was trying to come up with some reason he couldn't go. But she didn't have one. "No. . . . Go to your stupid carnival!"

"Sure you don't wanna come with us?" asked Carrot Boy.

I could have killed him.

"Not in a million years," said Emma. Then she went back to her dumb robot voice. "Luc-Bot! Watch movie! Terminate conversation!"

Phew. It was safe. Dusty was going to get to Zombie Nirvana. But first, Tanner Gannt was going to play in our band at Maren's party.

10.

A Verbal Agreement

We had two more band practices with Tanner Gannt. He wasn't late for either of them. Annie let him sing backup and even do one song solo. I didn't think he needed a solo, but I didn't say anything. Zeke still kept twenty feet away from him.

There were ten songs we could do for Maren's party. Capri wanted us to learn some new songs by famous singers and bands, but Annie said, "No! We are not a cover band. We only do original songs."

"We're going to Fancy Town!" said Zeke when

we got in the car to go to Maren's. She lived in a neighborhood where everybody had huge houses. She used to go to a private school called Ridgeview Academy before she came to Hamilton.

My mom dropped me and Zeke off an hour before the party started so we could set up. The rest of the band was already there. It was dark and the full moon was up, so I'd turned into a werewolf. I was glad I'd have my deep, gravelly, rock-and-roll voice. Tanner Gannt couldn't sing like *that*.

A grumpy lady on the front lawn of the house next door watched us unload. "If you play loud, I'm calling the police!"

I was going to quote Gram, who always says, "If it's not loud, it's not rock and roll!" But I didn't.

There was a purple van parked in Maren's driveway with a sign on it that said: MONTY THE MUSIC MAN—BEST DJ EVER! MUSIC FOR ALL OCCASIONS! WEDDINGS, BIRTHDAY, BACHELORETTE, BACHELOR, BAR MITZVAHS, BAT MITZVAHS, FUNERALS, MEMORIALS

"They hired a DJ, too?" said Capri.

"Maren's rich," said Dog Hots.

"No," said Annie. "Her *parents* are rich."

"She'll be rich someday," said Tanner Gantt.

Annie went to knock, and Maren's mother opened the door. She looked exactly like Maren, except taller and older.

"Hi, Ms. Nesmith," said Annie.

She gave Annie a strange look. "You're early. The party doesn't start for an hour. Come back in—is that a dog? Why isn't it on a leash?"

She was looking at me. Tanner Gantt laughed.

"He's not a dog," said Annie. "That's our singer, Tom."

I waved a paw.

"Hi, Ms. Nesmith. I go to school with Maren. I'm a Vam-Wolf-Zom. Maybe she's told you about me?"

She did a fake smile just like Maren's.

"Oh . . . yes . . . right . . . the special boy."

"It's a full moon so I'm a werewolf. But I won't bite anybody, I promise."

I've learned to say stuff like that because some people still think I'm going to bite them or eat them or drink their blood.

"What is all this equipment?" asked Ms. Nesmith.

"We're Conundrum," said Annie, proudly.

"You're *what*?"

"Conundrum!" said Zeke, pumping his fist in the air. "We're the band! Ready to rock your world!"

"Maren hired us to play at her party," said Annie.

"What on *earth* are you talking about?" said Ms. Nesmith. "I don't know anything about that."

"Oh . . . maybe you just forgot?" said Annie. "She called you when we were on the bus, and she said it was okay."

"And you're going to pay us," said Dog Hots, smiling.

"Maren did not ask me if she could have a band play," said Ms. Nesmith.

"Maybe she asked her dad?" said Zeke.

"Her father is not here."

"Maybe it's a surprise?" said Capri.

Annie was getting impatient. "We need to come in and set up our equipment."

Zeke held up the homemade wet suit he had made out of his raincoat and duct tape. "I brought a wet suit, Ms. Nesmith. Can I go swimming?"

Ms. Nesmith did another fake smile and said, "Stay right here. I'll be back shortly."

She shut the door in our faces.

"Rude!" said Annie.

"She's not gonna let us play," said Tanner Gantt. "Let's go."

"We are not going *anywhere*," said Annie.

Capri sighed. "I wanted to see her wiener doodle."

"I was looking forward to perusing the art collection," said Abel.

The front door opened. Maren was standing behind her mom.

"Maren, what do you have to say to your little friends?" said her mom.

"I shouldn't have asked you to play without getting permission," Maren said so quietly you could barely hear her.

"I hired a DJ. We don't need a band," said Ms. Nesmith.

"*What* . . . ?" said Annie.

"But why can't they play?" said Maren. "Daddy'll pay for it. I know he will."

"Your father is not putting on this party. I am."

Maren stomped off.

"I'm sorry, but your band can't play," said her mom. "You may come back in an hour." She started to close the door, but Annie put her hand out and stopped it.

"Wait a minute!" said Annie. "We've been practicing for this for two whole weeks! We even got a new bass player!"

"And I learned three more chords on the banjo," said Zeke.

"I bought a new outfit," said Capri.

Abel cleared his throat. "May I make a suggestion, Ms. Nesmith? Perchance we could play a shortened set, three or four selections, at an appropriate time of your choosing?"

"We do not need a band," she said, and closed the door.

11.

Secret Weapon

"I hate Maren!" said Capri.

"I hate her mom!" said Dog Hots.

"We should call our parents to come get us," I said.

"What?" said Zeke. "Aren't we gonna come back in an hour and go to the party? What about the doughnut tree?"

"I don't want to go to Maren's stupid party!" said Capri.

"She should still pay us," said Dog Hots. "Let's

call a lawyer. She made a verbal agreement. I saw that on TV."

I could tell Annie was thinking.

"We can still play this party," she said.

"How?" we all said at the same time.

Annie smiled at me.

"We have a secret weapon."

○ ○ ○

Annie knocked on the door again, with me standing next to her. Ms. Nesmith answered.

"I thought I told you children to come back later!"

I stared into her eyes. "Ms. Nesmith, we want to apologize."

"Fine! Now please go!"

I kept staring at her. "We really mean it. Don't I look sincere?" She looked down at me. "Look into my eyes and know that I am telling the truth. . . . Look into my eyes. . . . Listen to my voice. . . . You are feeling drowsy. . . . You are getting sleepy. . . ."

Her eyelids started to get droopy.

"Ms. Nesmith?" I said.

"Yes . . . ," she said softly.

"You are going to let our band play."

"I will . . . let . . . your band play."

Dog Hots whispered to me, "And remind her to pay us."

"And you will pay us."

She nodded. "I will . . . pay you."

"And play as *loud* as we want," said Tanner Gantt.

"And we can have as many doughnuts from the doughnut tree as we want," added Zeke.

I turned around. "Okay, you guys! Enough!" I turned back to Ms. Nesmith. "You will wake now."

I snapped my fingers. She smiled. A real smile
this time.

"Come in, Conundrum. Set up your equipment
in the tent next to the doughnut tree."

12.

Brave or Crazy?

We went inside the house. There were pictures of Maren all over the place, on every single wall.

"What is this?" said Annie. "The Museum of Maren?"

"Precious!" said Capri as Maren's wiener doodle dog ran up, barked at me, and started sniffing my leg.

Capri bent down to pet her. "This is the cutest dog in the world."

"And one of the most expensive," said Abel.

We went out to the backyard to set up. It was huge. Since it was February, they had a giant plastic heated tent over the whole yard, even the pool.

Zeke ran over to the woman setting up the doughnut tree. It was like a Christmas tree, with doughnuts hanging on it. "This is the most beautiful thing I have ever seen! I don't know which one I want! They all look amazingly amazing!"

"Later, Zeke. We have to get ready," said Annie.

We set up on one side of the pool. The DJ, who was on the other side, gave us a dirty look.

"Nobody told me there was going to be a band."

"We are a last-minute addition," said Abel.

"What songs are you going to play?" he grumbled. "We can't play the same ones."

Annie smiled. "Don't worry, we won't. We only play original songs."

The DJ looked relieved. "Original songs? Good luck."

○ ○ ○

Kids started arriving for the party. There were some from our class, but mostly it was girls from Maren's old school and her cousins. Two girls asked to pet me, which isn't entirely a bad thing. One girl saw me and screamed, locked herself in the bathroom and called her mom to pick her up.

There was a magician named Handsome Harry, who was bald and went around doing card tricks. Abel showed him some new moves.

A lady was drawing people's faces, and Zeke fell in love with her because she looked like the actress Keelee Rapose, who played Vacuum Girl.

The kids from our school were surprised to see Tanner Gantt.

Jason Gruber went up to Annie. "*Why* is he here?"

"We're trying him out as our bass player."

"Seriously?"

"Yeah. He's good."

Jason shook his head. "You guys are really brave or really crazy."

◦ ◦ ◦

A man came into the tent and said, "Where is she?!" He was tan and had long hair, and was wearing a white shirt that he hadn't buttoned very much. He looked like he went to the gym a lot and wanted people to know it. There was a lady with him that sort of looked like Tanner Gantt's mom, but younger and blonder and skinnier. Maren's mom didn't look happy to see him.

"You're *late*," she said.

"Traffic," he said.

"Daddy!" said Maren, running over to him. She jumped up for a giant hug.

"There's my beautiful birthday girl!" He kissed

her on the cheek and then put her down. "Maren, this is my new friend, Starling."

Maren looked at the lady and stopped smiling. "Hi."

"Happy birthday, Maren!" said Starling. "You're Aquarius, like me!" She gave Maren a hug, but Maren didn't hug her back. She just stood there with her arms at her sides.

Maren's dad looked over at us.

"I didn't know you were going to have a band, Mare."

Was he going to ask us to leave? Was I going to have to hypnotize him, too?

He walked over to us. "Hey! Vam-Wolf-Zom kid. Maren said you'd be here. Cool! Hey, can I jam with you guys? I'm a pretty good lead guitarist."

Annie was in the bathroom. Since she's the leader of the band, none of us knew what to do. But I said, "Uh . . . sure."

"Awesome! I'll go home and get my guitar!"

"Daddy, you just got here!" whined Maren.

"I'll be right back, babe!" he said. "Hang out with Starling."

Annie came out of the bathroom and we told her about Maren's dad. She didn't seem too excited. "Okay . . . I guess he could play on one of our songs."

13.

The Band Curse

It was time for us to play. Maren and a bunch of her girlfriends from Ridgeview were hanging out on the other side of the tent. They were looking at me and whispering. I could hear them with my super hearing, but they didn't know it.

"He is, like, a total freak," Maren said.

"How can you go to school with him?"

"Is he going to bite us?"

"He's not that bad," said a girl with light brown hair in white jeans.

"I think it's sad. I feel sorry for him."

"Is his band good?"

"No," said Maren. "I just invited them so you could see Tom."

I went over to Annie, who was tuning her guitar, and said, "I just heard Maren say she only asked us to play so her Ridgeview friends could see me."

"What? Really?" said Annie. I nodded.

Annie put down her guitar and walked towards Maren.

"Oh, hi, Annie. What do you want? I'm kinda busy right now."

"Did you invite us to play just so your friends could see Tom?"

Maren got fake upset. "What?! Oh my God! Are you, like, serious? That is so not true!"

"Good," said Annie. "'Cause if you did, this party would not end well."

Annie came back. "She said she didn't do it."

"She's lying!" I said.

"I know. But look, we practiced, we're set up,

we want to try out Tanner. Let's just do it. For us. Not her. Who cares about Maren anyway?"

"Okay," I said.

∘ ∘ ∘

Just before we played, Maren's mother went up to the microphone.

"Good evening, everyone!" She was doing her friendly nice voice. "I'd like to propose a toast to the birthday girl, my awesome daughter, Maren Shantelle Bouvier Nesmith, the most incredible person I have ever known!"

Annie rolled her eyes. "I guess her mom hasn't met many people."

Maren's mom kept going, ". . . and is absolutely gorgeous . . ."

"Which Maren had *nothing* to do with," said Abel.

". . . strong, fierce, powerful . . ."

"Who does she think Maren is? Wonder Woman?" said Zeke.

". . . kind, sweet, caring . . ."

"Maybe Maren hypnotized her mom," I said.

". . . incredibly brilliant . . ."

"She cheats on tests," said Capri.

". . . mega-talented . . ."

"At what?" said Dog Hots. "Being a stuck-up jerk and a liar?"

". . . the most amazing person on the planet . . ."

"I guess she's never heard of Malala Yousafzai," said Annie.

I looked over at Maren. Even she looked embarrassed. It bugs me when parents brag like that. I mean, it's nice to be proud of your kid, but it's ridiculous to do it like Maren's mother was doing.

Then she gave us the worst introduction ever.

"Now here are some of Maren's little friends who are going to play some fun music! Please be polite and listen to them. Here is: Come Some Drum!"

"It's Conundrum!" said Annie.

"We need a new name," said Zeke.

14.

Pizza Problems

We played our first song, "Spying," the one Annie wrote about me spying on her. I have to admit it's a good song. And it sounded really good with Tanner playing bass. But none of the kids danced. They just stood there staring at us.

We finished the song and only Starling and the girl in white jeans clapped.

Maren and four kids came up to us.

"Do you know 'I Love Pizza (More Than I Love You)'?" asked one kid.

"No, we don't," said Annie.

"Do you know 'I've Got a Headache in My Heart'?" said another kid.

"No," said Annie.

"Do you know 'I Texted You 10,000 Times' or 'Dance Face'?"

"No. We only play original songs."

"Do you at least know 'Let it Go'?" asked a girl.

"I do!" said Capri. She started playing it on the piano.

"Stop, Capri!" said Annie. "We're not a cover band."

"But we want to dance to good songs," said Maren.

"I told you we should have learned songs people know!" said Capri.

The DJ walked up with a big smile on his face. "Hey, guys. I can play *all* the songs you just asked for."

"Do it!" shouted Maren. The DJ went back and played "Dance Face." Every single kid started dancing, except us.

"Maybe our band is cursed," wondered Zeke.

"There's no such thing as curses," said Annie.

I wasn't so sure.

∘ ∘ ∘

I was starting to get zombie hungry. Luckily, after "Dance Face," Ms. Nesmith grabbed the microphone and asked, "Who's hungry?"

Two waiter people came into the tent, each carrying five big Bonini Pizza boxes. They set them down on a long table.

Maren's mom started flipping open boxes. "We have three pepperonis, two veggies, a vegan, gluten-free, no cheese, Hawaiian, and Grand Slam with everything."

The Grand Slam had garlic. Lots of it. I started to feel sick. I grabbed two slices of Hawaiian and a cherry soda and went outside the tent to get away from the smell. I sat down next to the garage.

I heard a familiar noise above me. The sound of wings flapping. I looked up and saw a bat flying by.

"Martha?" I called.

It was just a regular bat. I was half glad and half disappointed. I wanted to see Martha, but I also didn't want to get yelled at. I have to admit, I was curious about what happened with Darcourt, and how she got the book back. I guess I'd never know.

The tent door opened and the girl in white jeans came out with a plate of pizza. I hoped she wasn't going to ask to take a picture of me.

"Why are you sitting out here?" she said.

"There's garlic on some of the pizza. I'm allergic since I'm a vampire."

"I hate garlic too. I'm Amaryllis, Maren's cousin. I liked your song."

"I'm glad somebody did."

She sat down next to me and said, "Can I tell you something I've never told anybody before?"

"Uh . . . yeah."

"I wanted to be a zombie when I was little."

"Really? Nobody wants to be zombie."

"I was pretty weird. Then, I wanted to be a vampire when I was six. And then I wanted to be a werewolf when I was ten. So, you're basically all the things I wanted to be at the same time."

"Do you still want be those things?"

"No," she said, taking a bite of pizza.

"Me neither."

"So, are you, like, friends with Maren?"

I didn't know how to answer that. "Uh . . . well . . ."

"She's a major stuck-up pain in the butt."

We both started laughing.

"Yeah, she is," I said.

I saw Capri watching me from one of the tent windows. She looked bugged. Probably because we didn't listen to her and learn any songs that kids knew.

Dog Hots stuck his head out the door. "Tom! Maren's dad's back! He wants to jam!"

"I gotta go, Amaryllis."

"See you around," she said.

15.

100,000 People

I went back into the tent, where Capri was waiting at the door.

"Who was that girl you were talking to?" she asked.

"Amaryllis. She's Maren's cousin."

"Why'd you go out there together?"

"We didn't. I went outside because I had to get away from the garlic on the pizza, and then she came out too."

"What'd you talk about?"

"Stuff."

"What stuff?"

"I don't know, uh, she liked our song."

"Do you like her?"

I shrugged. "She was nice."

"Is she your new girlfriend?"

"What? No!"

Zeke ran up holding a giant red doughnut. "T-Man! They have cranberry doughnuts! This is the greatest day of my life!"

We went over to Annie and the rest of the band. They were talking to Maren's dad, who was plugging his guitar into Abel's amp.

"An original 1952 Fender Telecaster guitar," said Abel. "That is an excellent instrument."

Maren's dad nodded. "Tell me about it. This thing cost more than my Tesla!"

"Do you guys know 'Smells Like Teen Spirit' by Nirvana?" he said.

"No," said Capri and Annie.

"I can play it," said Tanner. "That's my mom's favorite song."

"Awesome!" said Maren's dad.

"I've never heard of it," said Dog Hots.

"Not a problem," said Abel. "I know the drum part."

"You play drums too?" said Dog Hots.

"When the need arises."

Dog Hots handed his sticks to Abel, who sat down at the drums.

"Is there a banjo part?" asked Zeke.

"Thankfully, no," said Maren's dad. "It's just guitar and bass and drums."

"So? What do we do?" I said, meaning me and Annie and Capri and Zeke and Dog Hots.

"Dance?" said Maren's dad. He went up to the microphone and yelled, "Let's get this party started! Who's ready to rock?"

Starling shouted, "I am!" Nobody else did.

He looked around for Maren. "Where's the birthday girl?"

She was standing in the corner of the tent with her arms folded. Her mom was next to her doing the same exact thing.

"This is for you, babe! Happy birthday!" he shouted into the microphone. "One, two, three, four!"

They started playing the song. Maren's dad sounded just like the guy who originally sang it. He was a pretty good guitar player too. Abel was amazing on the drums. I could tell Dog Hots was jealous. Kids started dancing.

Amaryllis came up to me, "You want to dance?"

"Uh . . . okay."

Capri made a weird noise and stomped off.

Annie started packing up her guitar.

Zeke asked the caricature lady to dance, but she smiled and said, "Thanks, sweetie. Ask me again in ten years."

"I will!" he said, and went off to dance by himself. He doesn't mind doing that. He does it a lot. Even when there isn't any music.

I was dancing with Amaryllis, but I kept looking at Maren's dad. He was acting like he was a big rock star performing in front of a hundred thousand people at a stadium, instead of in a backyard at his daughter's birthday party. He was acting like it was *his* party. I sort of felt bad for Maren, even though I didn't want to. It's weird how you can feel sorry for someone who isn't a nice person.

During his guitar solo, Maren's dad went crazy. He was jumping up and down, running around, and spinning in a circle. He looked dizzy and bumped into Tanner, who got slammed into Zeke, who fell on me and knocked me right into the swimming pool.

I was soaked when I got out and looked like a wet dog. Maren ran into the house crying. Her mom yelled at her dad and ran in after Maren. Starling patted his back as he kept saying, "What did I do?"

The police showed up because the neighbor had complained about the noise. They went away when Maren's dad said the party was over.

I shook myself dry and accidentally splattered Amaryllis with water.

"Sorry!"

She laughed and got me a towel.

We packed up our stuff and went out front to the driveway to wait for our parents. Capri was really quiet. She was probably still mad we hadn't listened to her.

"So? Am I in the band?" Tanner asked.

Annie looked around at all of us and then back at Tanner.

"Yes . . . but on a temporary trial basis."

○ ○ ○

If someone had told me a year ago that I would either be a Vam-Wolf-Zom or I would be in a band with Tanner Gannt, I would have picked Vam-Wolf-Zom. But I didn't have time to think about how weird it was. The next day was Operation: Rescue Dusty.

16.

The Rescuers

RESCUE DUSTY PLAN

1. Drive to the carnival with Carrot Boy
2. Get to carnival and tell him the real reason
   we are there
3. Find Dusty's trailer
4. Wait until carnival closes at 10 p.m. and
   sneak Dusty out of the trailer
5. Take Dusty to Zombie Nirvana
6. Go home

o o o

Carrot Boy pulled up to our house at four o'clock on Sunday. Emma stood in the doorway, watching us and shaking her head.

"Last chance to come, Emmer-Lemmer!" said Carrot Boy, leaning out the car window.

"No way, Luka-Dooka," she said.

Those were their new nicknames. I was so glad that Em-Bot and Luc-Bot and the robot voices were gone, I didn't care what they called each other.

"We're gonna have buckets of fun!" he said.

Just in case Emma changed her mind I said, "They have a Graviton ride and deep-fried chocolate doughnut bacon cheeseburgers!"

She gave me some major stink eye. When I was five and she was ten, we went to a carnival that had deep-fried chocolate doughnut bacon cheeseburgers. She ate one and then she went on a ride called Gravitron. It was like a big flying saucer, and it spun around super fast. She threw up *four* times at the carnival in the gross, smelly, disgusting porta-potties. Then, she threw up *three* times on the car ride back home, and *one* time running up the lawn to our house, and *one* time going up the stairs to her room. The next morning, she came downstairs and announced, "I will never go to another carnival as long as I live!"

We were safe.

"When will you be back?" she called from the door.

"Late," said Carrot Boy. "It's two hours away."

"Where is this stupid carnival?" she asked.

"It's in Clarksville, near Grover's Square," I said.

I didn't know it, but I'd made a huge mistake.

Emma's eyes got big, and she ran toward the car. *"Grover's Square . . . ?!* Are you serious . . . ?!"

My stomach got queasy. *"Yeah . . . why?"*

"They just opened a new outlet mall in Grover's Square! Luca-Dooka, I'm going with you!"

Why? . . . Why? . . . Why did I open my Vam-Wolf-Zom mouth?

I wanted to fall down to my knees and scream, *Nooooooooo!* like they do in movies. I didn't. I should have. It might have made me feel better.

Emma loves outlet malls, where everything's on sale. I bet she would live in an outlet mall if she could.

We had to wait twenty minutes while she put on more makeup and got dressed. She got in the car and said, "Drop me off at the outlet, you go to your dumb carnival, and then come pick me up at nine when the outlets close."

Emma wrecks everything.

Always.

17.

A New Plan

NEW REVISED RESCUE DUSTY PLAN

1. Drive to stupid outlet and drop off stupid Emma
2. Drive to carnival and find Dusty's trailer
3. Sneak Dusty out of the trailer without Boss Man or anybody else seeing us because the carnival will still be open because of stupid Emma
4. Drive Dusty to Zombie Nirvana
5. Drive back to stupid outlet and pick up stupid Emma
6. Go home

o o o

The two hour-drive was horrible. For the first hour, Emma sang along to an album by her new favorite singer, Feeta Reeba. Emma is such a bad singer that it should be against the law for her to sing. I sat in the back seat and tried not to listen, sipping the raw liver chocolate smoothie Mom makes for me to get my daily blood. It tastes much better than it sounds.

During the second hour, Emma made us listen to a podcast called "Outlet Shopping Commando Techniques for Fierce Fashionistas." I thought about different ways to get Dusty out of the trailer without people seeing us. It wasn't going to be easy.

Finally, we dropped her off at the outlet.

"Bye, Emmer-Lemmer!" said Carrot Boy.

"Pick me up right here at nine o'clock. Do not be late!"

o o o

It took us about fifteen minutes to drive to the carnival. There were rides with bright flashing lights and loud music blaring, and carnies trying to get people to play the games. It was crowded and noisy, with people walking around eating food and some carrying giant stuffed animals they'd won.

No one stared at me because they were too busy looking at carnival stuff. I had a hat pulled down low, and my black hoodie under it. I've learned to keep my mouth shut to hide my fangs. And even though my face is pale, I figure most of the time people just think I'm a goth kid.

The carnival smells were pretty intense for a Vam-Wolf-Zom. They had hot beef sundaes, deep-fried peanut-butter pickles, spaghetti and meatballs on a stick, caramel-covered cotton candy, fried jelly beans, ice-cream potatoes, and pancake burgers. I ate three deep-fried corn dogs wrapped in bacon so I wouldn't get hungry later. Carrot Boy had a s'mores sandwich.

"What ride do you want to go on first?" he asked. "Death Drop? Psycho Spinner? Yo-Yo Boomerang? Concussion?"

"Let's walk around and check 'em all out before we decide," I said.

What I wanted to do was find Dusty's trailer. We walked around for ten minutes and I didn't see it anywhere. Had Boss Man left early for some reason? Was this trip a total waste of time?

I went up to the least-scary-looking worker. He was running the game where you throw baseballs at dolls on a shelf to try to knock them over.

"Five balls, five bucks! Win anything on the top shelf! Give 'er a try! First ball's free!"

"No thanks. Where is the zombie exhibit?" I asked.

"It's gone."

18.

Allergies

Gone?" I said. "What do you mean, gone?"

"I mean gone. Ain't here no more."

"What happened?"

"Well, I'm not supposed to say, but last night, the zombie got too close to a kid, just about your age, and bit him!"

"Really . . . ?"

He smiled. He had about five teeth. "Nah! I'm pulling your leg! It's over next to Gravitron."

"Okay. Thanks."

"Don't let him bite you!"

As we walked over, I told Carrot Boy why we were really here. But I decided not to tell him everything right away.

"The reason I wanted you to come is that a friend of mine's here and I wanted you to meet him."

"Cool."

"His name's Dusty. He was a cowboy. He did rodeos."

"Awesome! I love rodeos! I wanted to do that, but I'm allergic to hay and horses and leather. Not a good fit for the Luc-ster."

"Well, anyway, he asked me to do him a favor."

We walked past Gravitron, and I saw Dusty's

trailer in the distance. Boss Man was out front, talking into a microphone.

"He's over there," I said, pointing at the trailer.

"By the zombie trailer?" he asked.

"No . . . *in* the zombie trailer."

"Huh?"

"My friend, Dusty. He's a real zombie."

Carrot Boy looked more confused than I had ever seen him. And I've seen him look pretty confused.

"What . . . ?"

"He's the zombie that bit me, but it was an accident. He doesn't eat humans. A guy named Boss Man keeps him tied to a chair in a dirty trailer. Dusty told me about a place called Zombie Nirvana where zombies can run around free. It's not that far from here. You're the only person I know who would help me take him there. Will you do it?"

Carrot Boy stared at me with his mouth hanging open. Then, he said, "Dude . . . dude . . . dude . . ."

How many times was he going to say dude?

"I will totally do that! I am in! Our glorious quest lies before us! Free the zombie!"

"Thanks!"

I was pretty sure he'd do it, but it was good to hear him say it. Carrot Boy was cool. Why did he date Emma?

"What's the plan, man?" he asked.

"Okay, we have to get Dusty out of the carnival without anybody seeing us—especially Boss Man. We gotta get him out by eight o'clock, so we can take him to Zombie Nirvana and pick up Emma by nine. Boss Man's gotta take a break sometime. That's when we'll do it. But first I want to go in and see Dusty."

19.

Meeting Dusty

See a real live, one hundred-percent-authentic zombie!" said Boss Man into a microphone, standing in front of the trailer. "No cameras or cell phones allowed inside! If you try to take a picture or video, we will feed you to the zombie and he's mighty hungry tonight! We will take a picture of you with the zombie for no additional charge! Do not miss this once-in-a-lifetime opportunity!"

Carrot Boy and I stood back and watched three teenage girls pay to go in. Boss Man went in with them. After a while, we heard the girls scream, and one of them ran out. The other two came out laughing, and Boss Man followed. We walked up to him.

"Two tickets, please," I said, keeping my head low in case he recognized me. He was in the zombie business after all.

Inside the trailer it was dark, except for a red spotlight shining on Dusty. His head was hanging down. He was tied to his chair behind a big sheet of thick plexiglass.

"If you think he's wearing makeup, think again. He's the real deal," said Boss Man, standing beside us. "We keep him behind a protective barrier so he can't bite you."

Boss Man banged on the plexiglass and Dusty looked up. I did a little wave with my hand. I could tell he was surprised to see me. He smiled.

"Hi, Dusty," said Carrot Boy.

I couldn't believe he said that! I could've killed him!

Boss Man leaned over. "What'd you just say?"

Carrot Boy was about to say something, but I said, "He . . . he . . . he said 'musty.' It's musty in here."

Boss Man grunted and picked up a greasy paper bag of hamburgers. "Wanna see him eat?"

"No," I said.

He ignored me and threw a hamburger at Dusty, who caught it in his mouth. Then, Boss Man picked up a long wooden pole.

"Listen, you look like two cool dudes. For five bucks, you can poke him with this stick. He gets real mad. Puts on quite a show."

"No, thanks," I said.

"Suit yourself," he said, putting down the stick and picking up a camera. "Stand on either side there for your picture, and say, 'Brains!'"

We didn't want to, but we did. "Brains!"

Boss Man walked out of the trailer to print the picture. I went up to the plexiglass and whispered to Dusty, "We're gonna get you out of here and take you to Zombie Nirvana."

Boss Man poked his head back in the door. "What're you doing, kid? Show's over!"

Outside, as I watched the photo come out of

the printer, I remembered I wouldn't show up in it because I'm a vampire. I reached out to get it before Boss Man could see. He grabbed my hand.

"Hey! Don't be touchin' that! You're gonna wreck my printer!"

"Sorry."

I looked down at the picture in the tray. You could see Dusty and Carrot Boy, but not me. I had to distract Boss Man.

"That's an awesome tattoo," I said, pointing at a dragon riding a motorcycle on his arm.

He looked down at his arm proudly. "It sure is."

I reached out for the picture again. "Can I have it?"

As he handed it to me, he looked down and said, "What the . . . I can see your friend and the Zom, but you're all blurry. . . ."

Did he know? What would he do?

"Dang it, kid! You messed up the picture grabbin' at it! Well, I'm not doing another one!"

I took the picture. "That's okay! Thanks!"

We walked away and went behind a frozen jambalaya stand.

"I'd like to poke Boss Man with that stick!" said Carrot Boy.

"Yeah, I know. Me too. Okay, we have to wait

until he takes a break so I can go in and get Dusty out."

"It's a long way to my car. Won't people notice a zombie walking through the carnival?"

That was a good question. I'd thought we'd be doing this when the carnival was closed, so nobody'd be around. We needed a disguise. We had to hide Dusty's face and get a sweatshirt or T-shirt. Luckily, there was a stand selling T-shirts. I bought an extra-large long-sleeved T-shirt that said, CARNY AND PROUD. I had to use all my money.

Now we needed a mask. Carrot Boy said he'd pay for it.

"Do they sell masks anywhere here?" I asked the T-Shirt Guy.

"Nope."

We *had* to get something to cover Dusty's face.

"We do not *sell* masks," said T-shirt guy, "but you can win one of them *lucha libre* wrestler masks at the High Striker game, over by the hot-fudge corn dog stand."

20.

The Prize

The High Striker is a game where you use a mallet like a big sledgehammer. You hit a rubber pad as hard as you can, so a metal disk slides up a tower and rings the bell at the top. I'd tried it once at a carnival and it only went up to ten. The top number was one hundred.

The lady carny operating High Striker had a buzz cut, six earrings in each ear, one in her nose, and was wearing a T-shirt with no sleeves that said I AM NICE. Behind her was a row of lucha libre masks in different colors on a shelf.

"How do you win one of those masks?" I asked.

"Hit the bell. Get a mask. Easy as pie."

"Give it a whack, Tom," said Carrot Boy.

"Maybe you should do it," I said. "You gotta hit it exactly right and be really strong."

Carrot Boy smiled. "You mean like a Vam-Wolf-Zom?" he whispered.

I am so dumb sometimes. Carrot Boy gave some money to the lady.

"Good luck, kid," she said with a smirk.

I picked up the giant mallet. I swung it over my head and down onto the pad. The disc went up and hit the bell so hard the bell broke.

The lady got really mad.

"You broke it!" she screamed.

"Sorry."

"How'd a pip-squeak like you do that?"

I shrugged. Sometimes that's the best thing to do when people ask you questions you don't want to answer.

"Now I gotta close up!" she yelled.

"Can I have my mask?"

She looked like she wanted to hit me with the mallet. She grabbed a silver and red mask and threw it at me.

◦ ◦ ◦

We went back behind the frozen jambalaya stand. Boss Man was still out in front of the trailer, talking into his microphone.

"Are you brave enough to behold a sight so strange, so horrifying, so utterly monstrous, you may have nightmares for the rest of your life?"

We waited and waited and waited. It was getting late. We'd barely be able to take Dusty to Zombie Nirvana and then make it back in time to pick up Emma.

"Look!" said Carrot Boy.

Boss Man was locking the trailer door. He put a sign up.

BACK IN FIVE MINUTES . . . STAY OUT OR DIE!

Carrot Boy stood guard in front to keep a look out for Boss Man. I snuck around the back of the trailer. I made sure no one could see and then I turned into smoke and slipped inside through the door crack. Dusty looked up from his chair as I changed back into me.

"Well now, you're a sight for sore eyes," he said.

"We've only got five minutes!"

I started to untie the ropes on his arms. Then, I noticed something I hadn't seen earlier. He had chains around his legs.

"Dusty, when'd he put chains on you?"

"Last week. He figured it looked scarier."

"Do you know where the key is?"

"Boss Man's got 'em."

It was over. We couldn't get him out. I'd have to leave him there.

"Dusty . . . I'm sorry, but . . ."

"Y'know, I reckon since you're a Vam-Wolf-Zom you're one strong feller?"

I forgot *again*! I pulled on the chains and they snapped apart in my hands.

"You're a regular Hercules," said Dusty.

He put the T-shirt and mask on as I unlocked the front door and peeked out.

"All clear?" I asked Carrot Boy.

"Affirmative. We are a go!"

I turned to Dusty. "Ready?"

"Let's hit the trail."

All we had to do was get out of the carnival and get to the car without anyone noticing we had a zombie with us.

21.

The Great Escape

The trailer was at the farthest corner of the carnival. We had a long way to go. The three of us walked down a narrow dirt path behind the games and rides, but Dusty couldn't walk very fast. I guess he'd been in the chair for such a long time that he was stiff.

"Sorry, I'm goin' at such a slow trot," he said.

"It's okay," I said.

We were almost to the exit gate when we saw Boss Man walking toward us, eating a slice of chocolate pizza. He might recognize Dusty, even

with the mask and T-shirt. We couldn't take a
chance.

"Turn around!" I said. "Dusty, get in the porta-
potty!"

We'd just passed three porta-potties. They
smelled really bad, like no one had cleaned them
for a week. I tried the door handle on the first one.

"Somebody in here!" said an angry voice from
inside.

We tried the next one.

"This is occupied!"

We tried the next one.

"Busy!"

They were all full.

Dusty hid behind one of the porta-potties just as Boss Man saw us.

"What're you doing back here?" he said. "This path is for carnival employees only!"

"Oh—uh—sorry! We got lost!" I said.

"Get back on the midway," he said, stuffing the last of the pizza in his mouth.

Somebody came out of one of the porta-potties and Boss Man went in. I motioned for Dusty to come. As we started to walk away, he stopped for a second.

"What's wrong?" I asked quietly.

"Could you do me one more favor?" Dusty asked.

"What?"

He whispered in my ear. I smiled and nodded. Carefully, I put my hands on the side of the porta-potty with Boss Man inside.

"One . . . two . . . three!"

I pushed the porta-potty over, door side down, so Boss Man couldn't get out. We heard a disgusting, sloshing, splashing sound from inside. The smell was so bad, I had to hold my breath.

Boss Man started screaming his head off.

"Hey! . . . What the— . . . Nooooo! . . . Help! Help me!"

We slipped out to the front gate and the parking lot, with Dusty laughing all the way.

22.

A Phone Call

Dusty got into the back seat of Carrot Boy's car and took off his mask. I sat up front and turned around to face him.

"You got the map?"

"Sure do." He handed it to me.

"It'll take us about forty-five minutes to get to Zombie Nirvana," I said. "We can drop you off and make it just in time to get back to Emma."

"Who is Emma?" asked Dusty.

"You don't want to know," I said.

Carrot Boy pulled out of the parking lot. "She's Tom's sister and my girlfriend. I'm Lucas."

"Pleased to meet you, Lucas. I'm much obliged."

Carrot Boy's phone buzzed in a holder on the dashboard. I looked at the screen and a picture of Emma popped up.

"Don't answer!" I said.

Too late. He'd already tapped the speaker button.

"Hey, Emmer-Lemmer."

"Luca-Dooka pick me up! Right now!"

"Emma, it's only seven thirty! You said nine!" I said.

"They closed the outlets!" she shrieked. "One of the stores' air conditioners blew up and it smells like a toxic apocalypse wasteland here!"

"But we're still at the carnival," I said, which was technically true.

"I! Don't! Care!" she yelled.

"Can't you wait?" asked Carrot Boy.

"No! Come! Get! Me! Now!" she yelled.

I had to think of something.

"Emma, take a taxi to the carnival and we'll meet you somewhere."

I figured she would come to the carnival, then we'd pretend we couldn't find her while we dropped off Dusty and went back to get her. She'd be mad, but she'd be madder if she saw Dusty. We'd never get to Zombie Nirvana.

"That sounds like a good idea, Emmer-Lemmer," said Carrot Boy.

"I'm going to die if you don't pick me up right now!" she screamed.

"I'll be right there," said Carrot Boy.

There was nothing I could do. Emma was going to meet Dusty.

23.

Emma Meets Her Second Zombie

I tried to tell Dusty about Emma on the way, but I couldn't say much with Carrot Boy right there. When we pulled up, Emma was standing on the curb under a streetlamp. Carrot Boy stopped the car and she yanked the door open.

"*What* took you so long?! I've been waiting here forever! Tom, get in the back seat. . . ."

She saw Dusty.

"Okay, Emma," I calmly said. "Don't get excited. Don't freak out."

"Did you win a zombie dummy at the carnival?" she asked. "It looks totally fake."

"This is Dusty. He's a friend. Who happens to be a zombie."

Dusty smiled. "Pleased to make your acquaintance, Miss Emma."

Emma screamed so loud that I thought all the windows in the car were going to shatter, but they didn't. She ran down the sidewalk, screaming the whole time. Carrot Boy got out of the car.

"I'll be back," he said. "I hope."

He ran after her.

"She seems a might upset," observed Dusty.

"My sister freaks out easily."

"Well now, it ain't every day you meet a zombie."

"True. But she lives with one."

We watched out the back window as Carrot Boy tried to calm Emma down.

Finally, after about fifteen minutes, they came back to the car.

"I am *not* getting in that car!" she declared. "Either *it* goes . . . or *I* go!"

"Where are you going to go?" I asked, seriously wondering what she meant.

"He won't try to eat you," said Carrot Boy. "He just had dinner."

"Sorry I spooked you, Miss Emma," said Dusty.

"Emma, we gotta get Dusty to Zombie Nirvana," I said.

"*We*? What do you mean 'We?' I'm not a member of the zombie rescue squad!"

After about ten more minutes of arguing, she got in the car. She sat jammed against her door, staring back at Dusty every few seconds.

"Now, Tom here told me a lot about you," said Dusty. "But he neglected to tell me you were so lovely."

Emma loves compliments. Even from zombies.

"Uh . . . thanks," she said, sort of smiling.

"And I sure do 'preciate y'all doin' this for me. Riskin' your lives and doin' a mighty big favor for a stranger. Wish I could repay you somehow."

I could tell Emma was thinking about something. She had that face she makes that kind of looks like a camel chewing.

"Hey," she said. "Do you think we can get an award of medal for doing this?"

"No!" I said. "You can't tell *anyone* about Zombie Nirvana."

She grumbled. "It is so totally unfair when you don't get something for doing something nice."

"You get to feel good that you did something good," said Carrot Boy.

"Yeah. I guess," she said. "But you can't put it on a shelf and show it to people."

"You wanna listen to the radio, Dusty?" asked Carrot Boy.

"That'd be right nice. Haven't heard music for quite a spell. You think they got any country music stations 'round these parts?"

Carrot Boy found a country station and Dusty sang along. He had a good voice. Much better than Tanner Gantt's. Then, a song came on that Emma used to sing, when she wanted to be a country singer for about a week. She started singing. It was so bad I bet Dusty wanted to go back to the trailer.

When she finished squawking he said, "Miss Emma, you got a voice I do not think I will ever forget."

"Aw . . . thanks, Dusty."

We followed the directions on the map and pulled off the highway and went down a road. I

could see something in the distance with my night vision: a big billboard in front of a chain-link fence with a gate and a wall behind it. We got closer, and the car's headlights lit up the sign.

WELCOME TO ZOMBIE ISLAND

ZOMBIES ROAM WILD AND FREE!

SAFE

"There it is!" I said.

"We made it!" said Carrot Boy.

"Took us long enough," said Emma.

"Well, sir," said Dusty, "I reckon that ol' zombie was right after all."

As we drove closer, Emma leaned forward toward the windshield.

"Wait a minute . . . look."

Some of the words on the sign had faded. Carrot Boy stopped the car and we all got out.

WELCOME TO ZOMBIE ISLAND
Come if you dare!
ZOMBIES Roam Wild and Free!
NO ONE IS SAFE
CAN YOU ESCAPE ALIVE?
Open: October 1st-Halloween

24.

Plan B

It wasn't a safe place for zombies. It was an old Halloween Haunt Maze that must have closed a long time ago. The zombie who told Dusty about it probably saw the sign from far away. I looked over at Dusty. His eyes looked more watery than usual. Carrot Boy started sniffling. My eyes got a little watery too.

Nobody said anything for a while. Then, Dusty quietly spoke, "That surely is disappointing."

"I'm sorry, Dusty," I said.

"Ain't your fault, Tom. Sorry you went to such a heap of trouble."

Emma asked the question everyone was thinking.

"Now what do we do?"

"Maybe we could take Dusty home and keep him in my basement?" said Carrot Boy. "My mom never goes down there."

"Lucas, look at me," said Emma, sternly. "You are *not* keeping a zombie in your basement."

"Thanks for the offer, Lucas," said Dusty.

I said, "Maybe we could . . ." But then I couldn't think of anything.

Emma sighed. "Well, *this* was a complete waste of time."

"Not cool, Emma!" said Carrot Boy. "How'd you feel if you were expecting to go to an awesome place, where, like, all your dreams would come true, and then you couldn't do it?"

"Excuse me?" she said. "That just happened to me! They closed Grover's Square Outlets before I could finish shopping."

"I'll be all right," said Dusty. "Let me off here. I'll just mosey on down the road."

"No way," I said. "I'm not gonna leave you here."

"Wait! I have an awesome idea!" said Carrot Boy.

"Is it as awesome as your put-him-in-the-basement idea?" asked Emma.

He ignored her and turned to me.

"You should bite him, Tom."

"What?!"

"Turn Dusty into a Vam-Zom. Then, at least he could turn into a bat and fly away or turn into smoke and hide from people better."

Emma said, "That idea is fifty percent crazy and fifty percent insane."

"I don't know what would happen if I did that," I said. "And he'd have to get blood every day."

Dusty scratched his chin. "Maybe I should just get on back to the carnival? Least there I know I get fed. Roof over my head. No chance of bitin' nobody."

"I'm not gonna let you go back to Boss Man!" I said.

And that's when we heard a voice.

"Don't move. . . . Stay where you are. . . . Just turn around . . . nice and slow."

25.

An Invitation

Behind us was a big man with a beard, wearing jeans and a plaid jacket. He was holding a long pole with a wire loop on the end.

"Is that an unfortunate you got there?" he asked.

"Unfortunate?" I said, not knowing what he meant.

"I prefer that word to *zombie*."

"Yes," I said. "But we're not going to let you hurt him."

"Don't want to hurt him," said the man. "Want to help him. What's his name?"

"My name's Dusty."

"Please to meet you, Dusty. And your name?"

"Tom. And this is Emma and Lucas. We thought this was a safe place for zombies."

"It is. But I'm particular on who I let in. Like to check them out first. My name's Bradley."

He pulled open the gate and we went inside. Behind the wall there was a barn, a little field, and a pond. You couldn't see any of that from the outside. Bradley waved at a zombie sitting on a bench, under a light, gnawing on a big turkey bone.

"Hey, Jordan! Got some new friends!"

The zombie smiled and waved and went back to eating his turkey bone.

"That's my dear brother, Jordan. He became an unfortunate awhile back. At first, I just took care of him. Then I figured I could take care of other unfortunates. All you need to do is feed them and make sure they don't get loose. Only rule is don't eat anybody. We're not too crowded—about twelve of us. We have shuffleboard, movie night, a swimming hole, and Saturday night dances. Did you know unfortunates are fine dancers?"

"O . . . kay," said Emma. "This is the weirdest thing in the history of weirdness."

A horse trotted out of the barn.

"You got a horse," said Dusty, like he didn't believe what he saw.

"Yes, sir," said Bradley. "You're welcome to

ride." "I sure would like to do that. Been a long time."

"Good. Just don't eat him."

A lady zombie in a yellow, flowered dress and cowboy boots peeked around the barn and smiled at Dusty. He smiled back.

"That's Myrtle Mae," said Bradly. "She plays a mean fiddle and sings at our square dances." He turned to me. "So, there'll be two of you joining us?"

"No, just Dusty," I said. "I'm only one-third zombie. I'm a Vam-Wolf-Zom."

"I've heard of you. Well, if you ever change your mind, we'll be here. C'mon in, Dusty. You folks should head on out now. The less activity around here, the less we get noticed."

Dusty turned to us.

"Well, I can't thank you all enough for gettin' me here."

"You're welcome," said Emma, who had done nothing but complain the whole time.

"Nice to meet you, Dusty. Glad Zombie Nirvana turned out to be real," said Carrot Boy.

"Me too, Lucas. Thanks for drivin'."

"Bye, Dusty," I said. "Hope you like it here."

"I reckon I will, Tom . . . thanks to you. . . . Happy trails."

He turned and walked off toward the barn.

○ ○ ○

Emma, Carrot Boy, and I began the long drive home.

"Thanks for driving, Lucas," I said.

"No problemo. That was awesome, dude. This was the greatest day of my life."

"What?!" said Emma. "I thought you said the first time we kissed was the greatest day of your life!"

"Oh yeah . . . ," he said. "Right. This was the *second* greatest day."

It *was* a pretty great day. Sometimes things work out and good stuff happens. Unfortunately, there was a lot of bad stuff coming.

26.

Auditions

T-Man, we gotta try out for the school play!"

"No, we don't, Zeke."

We were standing in front of a poster in the hallway by the main office.

"Capri and I are trying out," said Annie.

"Trodding the boards can be a worthwhile and enriching experience," said Abel. "Playing a character, a person unlike ourselves, gives us empathy and understanding for other viewpoints."

"I'm gonna do stage crew," said Dog Hots. "We

get to use power saws!"

"I think I'll do that too," I said. "I don't want to be in the play."

The last play I did was in third grade. It was called *Fun on the Farm*. It was the dumbest

TRY OUT FOR
THE SCHOOL PLAY!
THIS FRIDAY!
3:15 IN AUDITORIUM!

MAKE NEW FRIENDS!
MAKE THEATER!

OPEN TO ALL GRADES!

THE TITLE OF SHOW TO BE
ANNOUNCED IN DRAMA ROOM 104
SNACK PERIOD TUESDAY!

ENTIRE PRODUCTION PERSONALLY DIRECTED BY MS. LUBICK.

play ever written. I played a duck with one line: "You quack me up!" On opening night I forgot my line because I was watching Annie, who was playing a goose, and got distracted. Zeke, who was playing a pig, could tell I forgot. So he said, "Hey, Mr. Duck! Did you think I was funny when I fell in the mud?" And then I blurted out, "I quack you up!" Emma made fun of me for a week, saying, "I quack you up!" all the time until Dad made her stop.

I'm not a big fan of theater. Probably because Mom and Dad forced me to go to all the horrible shows that Emma was in. They were so boring, I fell asleep every single time. Mom would jab me in the side to wake me up when Emma had a scene.

When it was over, Mom would always say, "Tell your sister how good she was."

"But she wasn't good," I said. "You want me to lie?"

"No . . . But you can think of something nice to say."

I said different things over the years:

"Congratulations!"

"You did it!"

"Wow! I can't believe what I just saw!"

What I wanted to say was, *Emma, you're really bad. Please stop being in plays so I don't have to come see them.*

Emma isn't good at acting or dancing or singing, but she thinks she is. I don't think Emma's good at anything except complaining and shopping. Mom says that Emma just hasn't found what she's good at yet.

So, I definitely didn't want to be in the play, but I did want to be on the stage crew. Working the lights and building sets sounded interesting.

°°°

On Tuesday during snack period, the drama room was jammed with kids. Zeke, Dog Hots, Annie, Capri, Abel, and I stood in the back because all the chairs were filled up. Ms. Lubick was standing on the tiny stage. She's the tallest teacher at school and has long hair that she likes to swirl around a lot. Zeke is in love with her. I think that was the main reason he was trying out.

"People . . ."

She always called students "people."

"For this year's play, we shall be doing . . ."

She took a long, dramatic pause and looked around the room. "A musical!"

The drama kids went crazy, cheering and whistling and hugging each other. Some kids make fun of them for getting so excited about stuff, but in a way, I sort of wish I got that excited about something.

An eighth grader named Carolyn Haney stood on her chair and yelled, "Yes! Yes! Yes!"

She'd probably be the star because she was a good actor and singer and dancer. I didn't like her though. Whenever she passed me in the hall, she gave me weird looks and stayed ten feet away. Not too many people did that anymore, except Carolyn. And Maren.

Ms. Lubick went on. "And the name of the musical is . . ."

She took *another* long pause. Kids started guessing.

"Is it *Annie*?" asked Carolyn.

"Is it *Wicked*?" asked Bella Peek, another eighth grader. She had a great voice, and in my opinion was tied with Olivia Dunaway for Prettiest Girl at School. She said hi to me in the halls sometimes.

"Are we doing *The Little Mermaid*?" asked

Esther Blodgett, who was combing her long, red hair. You could tell she wanted to be Ariel.

"No, we're not," said Ms. Lubick.

Esther said a bad word, but not loud enough so anyone could hear but me.

"Is it *Matilda*?" asked Kaiden Verdon.

"No."

"Are we doing *Hamilton*?!" shouted Emily Zolten. "I've seen it twenty-three times! I know all the songs! Please say we are doing *Hamilton*!"

"I'm sorry, Emily," said Ms. Lubick, "we are not doing *Hamilton*."

Emily put her head down on the desk and started crying.

Drama kids are so weird.

"So, what is it, Ms. Lubick?" asked an impatient Carolyn.

Ms. Lubick took a deep breath and exhaled. Kids were sitting on the edge of their seats, waiting to hear.

"We shall be doing a spectacular, amazing, fantabulous musical called . . . *The Maiden and the Monster*!"

Nobody cheered or yelled or hugged. I got a bad feeling in my stomach.

"I've never heard of it," said Carolyn.

"Me neither," said Jared Kenner, another eighth grader, who'd probably be the other star.

"Has it been on Broadway?" asked Annie.

"Not yet! But maybe someday," said Ms. Lubick, smiling.

"Did you see it performed somewhere?" said Bella.

"No."

"Did you read it?" said Jared.

"No," said Ms. Lubick. "I wrote it!"

Annie said, "Uh-oh."

"What's it about?" asked Carolyn.

"It is about a handsome prince who turns into a horrible-looking monster and the maiden who falls in love with him."

"Isn't that *Beauty and the Beast*?" asked Annie.

"Perhaps a bit," said Ms. Lubick.

"Why don't we just do *Beauty and the Beast* then?" said Carolyn.

"I love that show!" said Jared.

Emily raised her head and said, "I know all those songs!"

Ms. Lubick shook her head. "No, no, no. Every school from here to Timbuktu does *Beauty and the Beast*. We are going to do something new! Go where no show has gone before! Because our story takes place in the future . . . in outer space!"

"Will there be robots?" asked Zeke.

"Yes," said Ms. Lubick. "A chorus line of singing and dancing robots!"

"Excellent!"

She held up a stack of papers. "I have the audition scenes here for you. Read and see what part you'd like to try out for. Auditions are Friday after school in the auditorium. Three fifteen sharp!" The warning bell rang. "Now get to your next period and see you on Friday!"

As everybody got up to go, she said, "Thomas? Could you stay behind for a minute? I'll write you a late note."

When we were alone, Ms. Lubick smiled and said, "I am very pleased you are auditioning for the show."

"Oh . . . I'm not going to audition."

She looked like I'd just run over her dog.

"Why not?"

"Well, I'm not really into acting. I want to do stage crew."

"But I've heard you sing in choir. You are very talented!"

"Well, I like to sing, but I don't act or dance."

"Let me tell you something: singers *are* actors.

When you sing, you are acting. I think you could do it, Thomas. I know you are only a sixth grader, but I know talent when I see it." She lowered her voice and got serious. "And the part is, dare I say, perfect for you."

"Which part?"

"The part of Sandrich, the poor, unfortunate, misunderstood . . ."

"Monster?" I said.

"I'm not saying you are monster. I would never say that. But you are unique . . . special. Who could understand the part better than you? You wouldn't even have to act."

"But . . . isn't acting all about pretending to be somebody else?"

She made a thinking noise. "Mmmmmm . . . yes . . . and no. A director must always cast the best person for the role. And by the way, our performance happens to fall on a full moon . . ."

"So I'll be a werewolf."

"Yes! You were born to play this part. . . . Well, not *born*, but you were bitten to play this part."

"Um, sorry, Ms. Lubick, but I just want to do stage crew. I have to get to third period."

She leaned forward. "Thomas . . . with you in the lead, we have a good chance of winning the Cannon County Best Middle School Production Award. I have never won it, but this is my year—I mean our year! Don't say 'no.' Promise me you will think about it."

I just wanted to get out of there, so I said, "Okay. I will."

I thought about it on the way to class for about five seconds. I didn't want to play a monster. I was a monster every day. I can't believe she even asked me to audition. But I was still going to sign up for stage crew with Dog Hots.

∘ ∘ ∘

"Are you trying out for the school play?" Emma asked at dinner that night.

"No," I said, eating my third chicken-pork-beef taco.

"Why not? I bet you'd . . . quack me up!" She laughed like she'd just told the funniest joke of all time.

"Emma!" said Dad. "What did I say would happen if you ever said that again?"

"Um . . . nothing?"

"No! You have to do the dishes for a week!"

"What?! That is cruel and unusual punishment! There's a statue of limitations on that punishment!"

"Emma, the correct word is *statute*, not *statue*," said Mom.

"Whatever. We agreed I could say it once a year. We even signed a paper."

"That's right," remembered Dad. "We did."

My family is so weird.

"You should audition, Tom," said Mom, who always wants me to try doing different things. "You'd have fun."

"I played Snoopy when I was in middle school," said Dad.

"We know, Dad," said Emma. "You forced us to watch the video."

"I had a great song!" He opened his mouth to sing.

Emma pointed at him. "If you sing that song, I will kill you!"

Dad kept his mouth open but took a bite of his taco instead.

"I'm going to be on stage crew," I said.

"That's probably a good idea," said Emma. "It's *super* hard to get cast in the shows. I was in them every year, of course. But Ms. Lubick is picky."

"Actually, she asked me to try out for the lead."

Emma dropped her taco. "The lead?! Are you *kidding* me? You're only in sixth grade! Nobody in sixth grade is ever the lead! What are they doing, *Beauty and the Beast*?"

"EMMA!" said Mom and Dad in their best You-Are-About-to-Get-in-Big-Trouble voices.

"Sorry," said Emma. "What's the musical?"

"It's called *The Maiden and the Monster*. Lubick wrote it. It's kind of like *Beauty and the Beast*, but it takes place in the future in outer space."

Emma sighed. "I would have been an awesome Belle in *Beauty and the Beast*."

Mom did a fake smile and said, "That would have been . . . unforgettable."

She and Dad and I looked at one another, grateful we didn't have to see it.

Emma started to sing the first song from *Beauty and the Beast*.

"If you get to sing, I get to sing!" said Dad.

They both started singing.

Mom and I got up and left the room.

27.

The Announcement

On Monday morning, everyone who auditioned for the play ran down the hallway to the drama room to see the cast list posted to the door. Kids were jumping up and down, hugging, screaming, a few were crying, two said swear words, and some walked away with their heads down. I worked my way up to the front to see.

Cast List
The Maiden and the Monster
Felice, the Maiden . . .

Carolyn Haney (understudy: Bella Peek)
Sandrich, the Monster . . .
Jared Kenner (understudy T.B.D.)

Jared was a funny kid who was always joking around. He was the tallest kid at school, and a lot of girls thought he was handsome. But he'd be wearing monster makeup in the show, so that didn't matter. I looked down the list to see who else I knew in the show.

Tara the Thief . . . Annie Barstow
Professor Daedelus . . . Abel Sherrill
Robot #3 . . . Zeke Zimmerman
Townsperson #7 . . . Capri Ishiboshi

"Excellent!" said Zeke. "I'm Robot Number Three! I get to carry a laser sword!"

"Congratulations, Annie," I said.

"Thanks. Why doesn't Sandrich the Monster have an understudy?"

"What does T.B.D. mean?" said Zeke.

"To be determined," said Abel. "No doubt, Ms. Lubick will decide at a later date."

"Townsperson Number *Seven*?" complained Capri. "I don't have any lines! That's a crummy, small part!"

Abel smiled. "As the great director Konstantin Stanislavski said, 'There are no small parts, only small actors.'"

"I'm not small!" said Capri. "I'm the second tallest girl in our class!"

o o o

On the way to the first rehearsal, Annie asked me, "Have you read the play?"

"Not yet," I said.

She looked around and lowered her voice. "It's not very good. I could write something better."

She probably could.

The actors and the stage crew sat in two different groups. Tanner was on stage crew too. It was kind of cool to be hanging out with seventh and eighth graders. Mr. Herman, the algebra teacher, was in charge of stage crew.

"The actors perform the show, but we build it. We're all important," he told us.

As Lubick walked by me, she whispered in my ear, "I am not giving up hope, Mr. Marks. Perhaps you will change your mind. You would be a fine understudy."

Jared, who was playing Sandrich, was fooling around, making jokes, doing funny voices.

"Settle down, Jared!" said Ms. Lubick. "We have a lot of work to do."

28.

A Surprise Phone Call

That night, I was in my room writing a history report on President Rutherford B. Hayes when my phone rang. I didn't recognize the number.

"Hello?"

"Howdy."

I knew that deep voice right away.

"Dusty! How are you doing? Are you okay?"

"Doin' fine, Tom. Zombie Nirvana is one heck of a nice spread. I just wanted to thank you for gettin' me here."

"Do you have enough to eat?" As a zombie, I know how important that is.

"Yep, just had some tasty fried chicken with Miss Myrtle Mae."

"Who's Myrtle Mae?"

"We met her when you dropped me off. She's the fiddle player. A real nice lady."

"Is she your girlfriend?" I sounded just like Emma.

Dusty chuckled. "Well, now, that remains to be seen. Let's just say I wouldn't mind. How 'bout you? You have yourself a girlfriend?"

"Well . . . it's complicated. I like a girl named Annie a lot. And I met a girl named Amaryllis at a party who was really nice. But there's another girl I like named Martha Livingston."

"That sounds like what some folks call a *conundrum*."

I laughed and told Dusty that was the name of our band. "Martha's older than me."

"How much older?"

"Two hundred and twenty-four years."

Dusty let out a long whistle. "That's a mighty long time in the saddle."

"That's in vampire years. In human years she's thirteen. She's the one who bit me. But she's mad at me, so I don't think it's going to work out."

I told him about leaving Martha in the middle of chasing Darcourt because I saw his carnival trailer.

"Have you told either girl how you feel?" asked Dusty.

"Not yet."

"Might be a good idea."

I decided to change the subject, so I told him about the school play.

"When's the big show?" he asked.

"Two weeks from Saturday."

"How're Emma and Lucas?"

"They're okay. They have dumb new nicknames. Mister L and Ms. E."

"Well, people in love do curious things."

I heard a voice in the background. "Hey, Dusty! You comin' to the dance or not?"

"That's Myrtle Mae. I gotta go. Call me anytime you get a hankerin'. And best of luck with your play."

"Thanks, Dusty."

"Happy trails."

29.

The Accident

For the next week, the cast rehearsed every day after school from three fifteen until five, while we worked on the set. One day Tanner was painting something on the floor of the stage. Mr. Herman and I were testing the spaceship that flew across on a wire. We started pulling the spaceship. It hit a spotlight that was attached to a bar, and the light fell.

"Look out!" shouted Mr. Herman.

I was on the other side of the stage, but since I

can move so fast, I jumped up and caught the light just before it hit Tanner's head. He gave me the same look he'd given me when I stopped Dennis Hannigan from beating him up. I had saved his life *again*. Now he owed me double. At least he said thanks this time.

"Someone rehang that light and make sure it is secure," said Mr. Herman.

"I'll do it," said Dog Hots.

He went up on the wooden walkway above the stage and hung the light. But I noticed he was staring at Bella Peek most of the time, so it didn't look like he did a very good job.

Carolyn acted like she was a big star on Broadway, but I have to admit, she was really good. Jared kept fooling around and didn't know his lines, so Lubick was always yelling, "Learn your lines!" Kiev Lanner kept asking Lubick if he could be the monster's understudy. Dog Hots kept staring at Bella Peek and walked by her any chance he got. Zeke broke his laser sword three times because he got so excited during the fight scene. Tanner didn't make fun of anybody.

But one week before the show, everything turned upside down. I was hooking up a strobe light on the side of the stage. It was for the scene where a spaceship flew across the stage. I was quietly singing one of the Monster's songs ("I Don't Like Mirrors") to myself. I'd heard Jared sing it a million times and it was stuck in my head. I didn't even know I was doing it until I heard Lubick's voice behind me.

"You have such a good voice, Tom."

I stopped singing.

"It is a pity you are not in the show." She sighed and walked away.

I did sort of regret not trying out for a small part.

The cast looked they were having fun. Maybe next year.

"Let's do the escape scene!" Lubick yelled.

Carolyn went onstage with the robot sentries, Zeke and two seventh graders.

"I will help you escape the planet, Princess Felice!" Zeke said in his robot voice.

Carolyn put her hand on Zeke's arm and said, "I have always depended on the kindness of robots."

Zeke saluted and walked like a robot in front of her to go offstage.

"Stop!" yelled Carolyn. "What is wrong with you, kid? Don't cross in front of me. You're blocking my light. The show is called *The Maiden and the Monster*, not the *Maiden and Robot Number Three*."

"Sorry," said Zeke. She always called him 'kid," even though he told her his name every day.

"Settle *down*, Carolyn," said Lubick.

Jared came onstage to do the next scene with Carolyn. He still didn't know his lines, so he tried to be funny and started saying Carolyn's lines.

"Hey, maybe we

should switch parts and I should play Princess Felice?" He thought it was hilarious. Lubick didn't.

"Jared! Everyone knows their lines except you. I will no longer put up with your fooling around! Do you want to be in this show or not?"

"Yes, Ms. Lubick," he said quietly.

"Then, at tomorrow's rehearsal, you had better know every single line *perfectly*. If you don't . . . you will be replaced!"

"By who?" said Carolyn. "He has no understudy."

Lubick didn't answer her. "People, I have a small rewrite for the footbridge scene, which we're rehearsing tomorrow."

She handed a printout with the new scene to everybody. Annie, who is The Fastest Reader in the World, finished first.

"Whoa," she quietly said.

Other people started saying "What?!" "Did you see this?" "O.M.G.!"

"Carolyn and Jared have to kiss!" said Zeke.

"Quiet, Mr. Zimmerman," said Lubick.

Esther Blodgett grabbed Carolyn's arm, "Are you really gonna kiss him?!"

"Of course. It's part of the play. I'm a professional. I played Annie in *Annie* at the Circle Community Playhouse."

She's told us that a million times.

"Did you have to kiss somebody in *Annie*?" asked Esther.

"No. But I had to hug Sandy the dog. And he smelled. Actors have to kiss in shows all the time. It's no big deal."

Everyone knew that she had a crush on Jared.

° ° °

The next day at rehearsal, Lubick said, "People, may I have your attention, please. I do not want to hear any laughter, giggles, or comments during this scene. You are not elementary school children. You are middle schoolers and I expect you to behave as such."

They started doing the scene. Jared still didn't know some of his lines. Lubick kept stopping him and making him start over, so they hadn't gotten to the kiss yet. After five times she said, "Jared, what did I say to you yesterday?"

He smiled and said, "That I was the greatest actor you've ever seen?"

"Jared!"

"Sorry, Ms. Lubick, I promise I'll know my lines by the time we do the show."

Lubick stood up.

"Come with me, Jared."

The two of them walked out of the auditorium. Five minutes later, Lubick opened the door and poked her head back in.

"Thomas Marks, will you come out here, please?"

I went up the aisle and into the lobby. Jared wasn't there. Lubick put her hands on my shoulders.

"Tom, I need your help. The cast needs your help. The show needs your help. The school needs your help. The *theater* needs your help. Will you do it?"

30.

T.B.D.

Attention, people!" said Lubick. "Jared Kenner is no longer in our show. The part of Sandrich will now be played by Thomas Marks."

"Whaaaaaaat?!"

"Is she serious?!"

"Excellent!"

"He's a sixth grader!"

"Not fair!"

"He won't need any makeup."

"I was gonna make that joke!"

"Too late."

I could hear everything they said whether they wanted me to or not.

"Quiet!" said Lubick. "We will begin where we left off. Act Two, Scene Seven."

Carolyn, who looked very serious, asked, "Can I talk to you privately, Ms. Lubick?"

"Yes, but make it quick."

They went over to the other side of the stage. I pretended to look at the script while I listened to them.

"You can't have Tom be Sandrich," whispered Carolyn.

"Why?"

"You just can't."

"You have to give me a reason, Carolyn."

"He's . . . he's . . ."

"He's *what*?"

"He's . . . he's weird . . . he's not normal . . . he's a Vam-Wolf-Zom."

Lubick got super serious. "Carolyn, do you know what this play is about? The whole point of the show is that physical appearances do not matter. It's what's inside a person that counts."

"I know . . . but do I have to kiss him?"

"Carolyn isn't kissing Tom, Felice is kissing Sandrich. There is a difference. You are acting. It's not a real kiss."

"But . . . he's a real monster."

"I am ashamed to hear you say that. Tom is not a monster."

"Yes, he is. He's a vampire, a werewolf, and a zombie! He's three monsters."

Everybody was watching them. Lubick pulled Carolyn farther away, but I could still hear.

"Carolyn, just try the scene. Get into character and I think you will find it is no problem at all."

Carolyn stood there for a moment and then said, "Okay . . ."

"Good girl." Lubick came back onstage. "Places! Let's begin!"

Carolyn walked over to where I was, but she didn't look at me. Instead she looked over my head. I was holding my script, even though I knew most of the words since I'd heard them a million times.

She cleared her throat and said, "Before you

depart, Sandrich, I must do something I have wanted to do for a very long time."

"Save the Gorlops?" I said.

"No . . . kiss you."

"You would kiss a creature such as I?"

I was about to get my first kiss. It wasn't the way I thought it would be. Carolyn was pretty, but I didn't like her. And she thought I was a monster. I always hoped my first kiss would be with Annie. I stood there looking at Carolyn, waiting for her to kiss me, when all of a sudden she turned away.

"I can't do it!"

"Carolyn, what did we just talk about?" said Lubick.

"He's a . . ."

She looked at me and made a face like she smelled something bad.

"He's a *what*? said Annie, watching from the wings.

"I'm not going to do it," said Carolyn.

"I thought you were a *professional actress*," said Annie.

"Quiet, Annie," said Lubick. "Let me handle this."

"I am," said Carolyn. "But . . ."

"But what?" said Annie. "You didn't say anything when you had to kiss Jared."

"That's because Jared's not a you-know-what! I'd like to see you kiss Tom!"

"Let's everyone settle down," said Lubick.

Annie walked over to Carolyn. She was looking at her like she was gonna punch her. But she didn't. She turned and grabbed my face with both her hands and pulled me toward her.

She kissed me.

On the lips.

Zeke clapped.

Everyone watching went "Ooooooooooo!"

Our kiss ended and Annie turned to glare at Carolyn. "What is so freaking hard about that?"

I liked that my first kiss was with Annie, but I wish it hadn't been in front of twenty-seven kids and a teacher.

"All right, Annie," said Lubick. "You've made your point. Please sit down."

Annie sat down.

But it wasn't over.

Capri stood up, came over to me and said, "Yeah, Carolyn! What's the big flippin' deal!"

Capri kissed me.

On the lips.

For *twice* as long as Annie had.

I love theater.

31.

The Play Will Go On

Carolyn burst into tears and shouted, "I quit! I'm not doing this stupid show!" She ran offstage, up the aisle, and out of the auditorium. Her two best friends, Cecily and Gwendolyn, ran after her. They were crying too. People cry a lot in drama.

Ms. Lubick cleared her throat and said, "Things like this happen in the theater, but the show must go on. And it will. Bella Peek, you will take over the part of Felice. Unless that is a problem?"

Bella stood up and walked over to me and smiled, "No problem at all."

o o o

I called Dusty that night to tell him about getting the part.

"Congratulations, Tom. I was in a school play once, but I didn't get to kiss a girl. I played a cactus."

"I'm kind of nervous. I don't know if I can learn the part in one week."

"I reckon if you set your mind to it, you can do it."

"I hope so."

"Sure wish I could see that show. But I figure people'd get all riled up if a full-on zombie was sittin' in the audience."

"Yeah, probably."

"Say, you got Lucas's phone number? I'd like to thank him again for helpin' me."

I gave him Lucas's number.

"Much obliged, Tom. Let me know how the show goes. I'll be thinkin' about you."

o o o

The next day at rehearsal Lubick said, "I want to run all of Sandrich and Felice's scenes so Tom and Bella can get up to speed."

We got through all the scenes and then it was

time for the kissing one. Before rehearsal, Abel
had given me a toothbrush, toothpaste, and some
mints. He keeps all sorts of stuff in our locker.

Bella and I were about to start the scene.

She smiled and said, "You smell nice."

"Thanks." I have to remember to always listen
to Abel. Then I brought up something I'd been
worrying about. "Bella, on the night of the show,
it's going to be a full moon. I'll turn into a werewolf."

"I know," she said.

"Have you seen me when I look like that?"

"Yeah. I saw you backstage at the Winter
Show when you were getting into your snowman
costume. You sort of looked like my dog, Xavier."

"Your dog?" I didn't want to hear that.

She could tell. "I mean that
in a nice way," she said,
laughing. "He's a cutey. I
kiss him on the nose."

Was she going to kiss
me on the nose?

We started the scene.

I said my line. "You
would kiss a creature
such as I?"

We kissed. She had

to bend down because she's taller than me. I didn't mind.

I had now kissed three different girls in less than twenty-four hours. I was seriously thinking about becoming an actor when I grew up.

After rehearsal, Dog Hots said, "You are so lucky! What's it like to kiss Bella Peek?"

I shrugged. I figured that was the best answer.

Later, Capri came up to me and said, "Did you like kissing Bella Peek?"

I shrugged again.

o o o

For the rest of the week, I worked really hard to learn my part. I started to get excited about doing the show. Then, all of a sudden, it was Friday night. Showtime.

I had a big early dinner of steak and roast beef so I wouldn't be zombie starving during the show. I went through the living room where Emma was watching a movie called *Perfect Proposal* for the millionth time.

"I have a serious question, Tom. Is the show funny? Are you going to . . . *quack me up?*"

"I heard that!" yelled Dad from the kitchen. "Dishes for a week!"

I went upstairs. I wanted to go over my lines

again. The show was at eight, and we had to be at school at seven o'clock.

When I walked into my bedroom, I saw something I didn't want to see.

A vampire with long red hair sitting at my desk.

Martha Livingston had returned.

32.

Blackguard

The moon had come up, so I was a full-on werewolf. I tried to act super casual, like I hadn't left her to face Darcourt alone, and she'd just dropped by to say "Hi."

"Oh. Hey, Martha."

She didn't say anything.

"How are you doing?" I asked.

She just stared at me with her green eyes.

"Um . . . I thought you said you didn't want to see me again?"

She kept staring.

"Are you . . . thirsty?"

She narrowed her eyes.

"Is that a new dress?"

She spoke. Quiet at first, but with each word her voice got louder. And scarier.

"You coward . . . you traitor . . . you blackguard! . . . Rotter! . . . Cad! . . . Shabaroon!"

I didn't know what some of the words meant, but I knew they weren't compliments.

"Martha, I am really sorry I left you to go see the zombie, but I—"

"Left me? You deserted me!"

"I didn't desert you."

"You walked out on me!"

"I didn't walk out on you. Technically, I flew away."

"Fiddlesticks! You abandoned me and left me to face Darcourt alone. Give me one good reason that I should not suck your blood dry and destroy you?"

"Uh, well . . . it would be gross and disgusting?"

She stood up from the chair and came toward me. I backed away.

"Wait! You said you never wanted to see me again! You sent me that text!"

"What text?" she said, looking confused, but still mad. "I sent no text!"

"Yes, you did! Look! I'll show you!"

I grabbed my phone and scrolled back to find her text.

"I did not send this."

"Well, how was I supposed to know that? Who sent it?"

She was silent for a moment and then said, "'Twas Darcourt sent this. He inquired about you when I found him."

"But why would he send that text?"

"So you wouldn't come looking for me. As if you *would*!"

"I did go look for you!"

Martha didn't look like she believed me. I

decided to change the subject. "So, what happened?"

She sat on the edge of my bed and took a deep breath.

"After you *deserted* me, I flew after Darcourt down a dirt road off the highway. I changed to my human shape and demanded that he return the book to its rightful owner. He sneered and said, 'You're going to have to take it from me, Livingston.' I replied, 'Then I shall.'"

"Did you fight him?" I asked.

"I did."

"Who won?"

"He did. . . . Perhaps, if I'd had assistance from, oh, let's say a Vam-Wolf-Zom, who possesses many powers, he would not have! And so, Darcourt has the book."

"I'm really sorry, Martha. . . ."

She sighed. "I thought we were friends, Thomas Marks."

"We are."

"Are we? As my friend Benjamin Franklin said, 'A false friend and a shadow attend only while the sun shines.'" She looked out the window. "Friends don't desert friends in times of need."

"Well . . . friends don't turn friends into vampires," I said in my defense.

"We were not friends when I first saw you asleep at your grandmother's. You were my dinner."

"I'll bet if *you* were a Vam-Wolf-Zom you'd want to meet the zombie who bit you."

"Perhaps," she admitted.

"And after I talked with the zombie, I *did* go look for you. I found a piece of your coat, some of Darcourt's fur, and a page of the book. I looked for a long time, but I couldn't find you."

"And how was your momentous meeting with the zombie?" she asked.

I told her about Dusty and how I went back to help him escape to Zombie Nirvana.

"I am impressed and surprised. I did not think you were capable of performing such a worthy and selfless deed. I shall give you a chance to perform another."

"What do you mean?"

"During my altercation with Darcourt I was knocked unconscious. When I awoke, he was nowhere to be seen. I flew off to find him, but the trail had gone cold. I searched for weeks in vain. He is quite skilled at the art of disappearing."

"Why didn't you ask me to help?"

"I had no desire to cast my eyes upon you!"

"So, why are you here?"

"Yesterday, I learned that Darcourt is meeting with his pack to present the book at their semiannual Council of Werewolves."

"Why didn't he show it to them right away?" I asked.

"For such a rough and tumble assemblage of creatures, they are sticklers for formality. Now, there is only one way to infiltrate his pack and get the book back. And only one person who can do it."

I didn't like the sound of this. She went on.

"You are a werewolf. And though you do not deserve it, you are getting a chance to redeem yourself."

"What does that mean *exactly*? Redeem yourself?"

"Make amends. Right a wrong. So, you will go to the meeting, ask to join Darcourt's pack, go through the initiation, procure the book, and escape."

"That's all I have to do?" I said sarcastically.

"Yes. 'Tis a clear and simple plan."

"Why do I have to do *everything*?"

"Because you told Darcourt where you hid the book! This is your fault!"

I couldn't argue with that.

She stood up from the bed. "They are meeting at Oak Glenn. It is not far from here. Less than an hour's time, if we fly quickly. Are you ready?"

"What do you mean?"

"Thomas Marks, has your brain been rattled? Must I explain the meaning of the word ready? Come! We must depart with great haste!"

"What? No way! I can't go tonight!"

"And why *not*?" she said through gritted teeth, her fangs showing for the first time.

"I have a show tonight. I'm the lead part in the school play."

She did a Maren Nesmith Fake Smile. "Well! That's quite an accomplishment! Congratulations! I'm so happy for you!"

Then she yelled at me.

"You dare think for an instant that I will allow you to perform in a trite, trivial, inconsequential middle school play while the fate of the entire vampire world rests in your hands?"

"Uh . . . no?"

"If you refuse to come with me, I shall fight you to the death!"

"But wait . . . If I'm dead I can't get the book back for you."

"It's a figure of speech!"

She was serious. I wasn't sure what she'd do. Maybe she'd go bring back an army of vampires.

"Okay, but I have to be at school by seven o'clock."

"We shall only return when we have the book. Not a second sooner. Come!"

Then I thought of something. "Wait, won't Darcourt recognize me?"

"We shall change your appearance."

"How?"

"Dyeing your fur another color."

"But what about my scent? He'll smell me."

"Easily remedied with perfume. Now we must get to it. Have you ever dyed your hair before?"

"No . . . but I know someone who has."

33.

California Sunset

Over the years Emma had dyed her hair black, red, blond, green, purple, and pink. She never throws anything away, so I knew she'd have some old hair dye somewhere. I made Martha stay in my bedroom and snuck into Emma's room while she was still downstairs watching the movie. It was a total mess, as usual. I found some perfume called Ode to Boy on her dresser and put it in my pocket.

The hair dye was in one of the drawers of her makeup table, where she spends three hours a day. It was called California Sunset, and I hoped it would be blond. I brought it to the bathroom and started to get ready.

'WHAT ARE YOU DOING?!" Emma was standing in the doorway.

"I . . . I . . . I forgot. I have to dye my fur for the play." I held up the box. "Can I use this? What color is it?"

She grabbed the dye box from me. "It's blond. Why do you have to be blond?"

"Um . . . there's a line in the show where they say, "Your fur is so nice and blond."

I'd have to tell her someone forgot to say the

line when she didn't hear it in the show. That is, if I got back in time to do the show and didn't get eaten by a pack of werewolves.

"I'll help you dye your fur," she said.

"Really?"

Sometimes, once or twice every two years, Emma does something helpful. It's always surprising. I told her to just do my arms, hands, and face, since that's all that would show. She painted the dye on my fur with a little paint brush. It was gross. My fur came out bright yellow.

Emma laughed. "You look like a giant baby chick."

I didn't have time to fix it. I had to get going.

"Tell Mom and Dad I'm going to Zeke's house to run my lines. His mom will take us to the show."

"You don't want to run lines with me? I'm, like, practically a professional actress."

"Uh . . . next time!"

I went back to my room.

"I have never seen a yellow werewolf before," said Martha. "Quick! Give me the perfume, so I may douse you and disguise your scent."

She opened the bottle. I could smell it right away.

"Yuck! It smells like bubble gum, baby powder, and strawberries."

"It shall do the job."

Now I was a smelly yellow werewolf.

"Martha . . . Do you think we can pull this off?"

"We must. Let us go."

"Okay, but we really gotta try to be back by seven for the play or my teacher, Ms. Lubick, will kill me."

"Your teacher is the least of your worries, Thomas Marks. . . . Many things could kill you tonight."

"Oh great! This sounds like so much fun! I am so glad you bit me and started all this!"

"Who let Darcourt get the book?"

"If you hadn't lent it to me none of this would have happened!"

"Let us not waste time arguing."

We changed into bats. My fur was yellow, but my wings were black. We flew out the window and into the night sky.

34.

Burnt

Follow me. I know the way," said Martha as we flew down the street.

"Me too. I camped at Oak Glenn once, when I was a Boy Ranger."

She looked over, surprised. "*You* were a Boy Ranger? I am shocked."

"Just for one weekend. We camped at Oak Glenn. They made us get up in the middle of the night and do a midnight hike. We had to sing this dumb song. *We like, like, like, to hike, hike, hike.*

I quit the next day. Anyway, how do you know where the pack is meeting?"

"I have an informant. A spy, if you will, within the pack."

"How'd you get someone to be a spy?" I asked.

"I saved a werewolf's life once. A long story for another time. They owe me."

"Can't they get the book back for you?"

"No."

○ ○ ○

We flew for about half an hour before we got to the forest. We were low—just above the treetops.

"I smell smoke," I said. "Like a campfire."

In the distance we could see a clearing in the woods. There was a small fire burning in a pit surrounded by rocks. Standing around the fire were three adult-sized werewolves. They were like me: human-shaped with fur. One had white fur with gray paws, one had a black stripe of fur in the middle of its brown head, and one had bright golden colored eyes. Darcourt wasn't there.

I whispered to Martha, "They're three of them."

"I assure you I am capable of counting."

"You don't think we'll have to fight them, do you?"

"I have no intention of fighting. We are here to steal the book by stealth. Use your brain, not your brawn. And remember, they also have acute hearing and sense of smell. We must land on a branch high above them and stay downwind."

The werewolves were facing the fire, with their arms raised toward the flames. Each one held a long, thin, silver rod. I figured they were probably about to start performing some ancient deadly werewolf ritual. We flew closer.

"Don't let the marshmallow burn!"

"I like it burnt! It tastes better!"

"No, it doesn't! You want it golden brown, not black!"

"Don't tell me how to make s'mores!"

"I've been making s'mores since before you were a pup! I'm an expert!"

"Oh yeah? Well, take a look, Mister S'mores Expert, your marshmallow just fell in the fire!"

Gray Paws laughed, and Gold Eyes said one of Tanner Gantt's favorite swear words.

I couldn't believe it. These scary-looking werewolves were making s'mores? I didn't feel as worried about getting the book back. We landed on the top of the tallest tree, as quietly as possible.

"Where are the graham crackers and chocolate?" asked Gray Paws.

"I thought you were bringing them," said Gold Eyes.

"It was your turn!" said Gray Paws.

"I brought them last time!" said Gold Eyes.

"Are you telling me we have no chocolate or graham crackers?"

"Quiet!" said Stripe. "Where is Darcourt?"

"Do you think he *really* has the book?" said Gold Eyes.

"He'd better or we'll roast him over the fire!" said Stripe.

"Nice and brown!" said Gray Paws, tossing a marshmallow into his mouth.

"No! Burn him to a crisp!" said Gold Eyes.

"I'd like him medium rare," said Gray Paws.

I whispered to Martha, "Do werewolves eat werewolves?"

"They eat *anything.*"

I guess these werewolves were scarier than I thought.

35.

Missing

I noticed three motorcycles parked behind a tree. They looked just like Darcourt's. Why wasn't he there yet?

"Which one is the spy?" I whispered to Martha.

"It is safer if you do not know," she whispered back.

"Why?"

"Suppose you were captured and tortured to reveal that information?"

"What?! You didn't say we might be tortured?"

"Things happen. . . ."

The smell of the toasted marshmallows rose up to us.

"Those marshmallows smell really good."

Martha glared at me. "You said you ate a large dinner."

"I did, but I didn't have any dessert."

"We are not here for dessert!"

"Did you hear something?" said Stripe below us.

"No. . . . What?" said Gold Eyes.

"Sounded like someone whispering," said Stripe.

Before they could look up, there was a noise in the distance. A motorcycle. I sniffed. It was Darcourt's scent, and it was getting closer. He pulled up on his motorcycle in human form and parked it near the other ones.

"You're late, Darcourt!" said Stripe angrily.

Darcourt got off his motorcycle and smiled. "Where are your manners? No 'Hello, Darcourt, old buddy! Good to see you! You're looking handsome as ever!'"

"*We* all managed to get here on time," said Gray Paws.

"Were *you* being tailed by V.W.H.W.D.S.?" asked Darcourt.

"What's that?" asked Stripe.

"The Vampires Who Hate Werewolves Death Squad."

Gold Eyes looked scared. "What? Is there such a thing?"

Darcourt grinned. "Who knows?"

"Let us get to business," said a serious Gray Paws. "Where is the book?"

"Keep your fur on. I got it. Any s'mores left?"

"No," said Gray Paws, scowling at Gold Eyes. "*Someone* didn't bring graham crackers or chocolate! So, it's just toasted marshmallows."

"Darcourt, do you like yours burnt and blackened and covered in ash?" said Gold Eyes.

"Stop with the marshmallows!" said Stripe. "Let us see the book."

Martha leaned closer to me and whispered. "Fly back fifty yards and transform to wolf. Wait until you see the book, and then approach the group. When you have sufficiently distracted them, I shall swoop down and grab it."

"Then what do I do?"

She rolled her eyes. "Sing a campfire song. No! Change to a bat and fly away. Just make certain you see the book before you do anything."

"Okay . . . but what if something goes wrong?"

"Thomas, must I remind you *again* that you have the combined strength of a vampire and werewolf, plus the near indestructibility of a zombie?"

"Hey, I've never fought four werewolves. They don't teach that in sixth grade. Have you?"

"No. But werewolves cannot fly. Follow the plan and all shall be well. Now go. And good luck."

I flew about fifty yards away, landed, and transformed back into a werewolf. I really hoped this would work.

36.

Howdy

The werewolves were still arguing.

"Show us the book!" said Stripe.

Darcourt smiled. "Dude . . . chill. Relax."

"I don't think he has it," said Gray Paws.

"Show us!" demanded Stripe.

"Okay, okay," said Darcourt. "You guys are so impatient."

He reached into one of the leather saddlebags on his motorcycle and pulled out a small package wrapped in brown paper and tied with string.

"*A Vampiric Education* . . . This book teaches

us their secret ways. We will be able to overpower vamps once and for all. And the Society of Shape-Shifters will pay us some major money for it."

"You have read it?" said Stripe.

Suddenly, Darcourt raised his nose in the air and sniffed.

"We're not alone!"

The werewolves growled and began to look around.

Darcourt sniffed again.

"I smell . . . bubble gum . . . baby powder . . . and . . . raspberries?"

Gold Eyes looked confused. "Why would a baby be chewing gum and eating raspberries out in the woods?"

I knew Martha put on too much perfume!

"I smell me some wolf," said Darcourt, putting the book down on top of his motorcycle seat.

"How many?" said Stripe. "Is it a pack? Anyone we know?"

"Could it be the Fur Balls? The Crimson Claws? Los Lobos?" guessed Gold Eyes.

The werewolves tipped their heads back, raised their snouts, and sniffed.

"Wait a sec," said Darcourt, sniffing a third time. "I also smell . . . bat."

Had the wind changed? Could he smell Martha?

"Natural bat? Or vampire?" said Stripe.

I had to make my move. We had to get the book before we lost the element of surprise.

"Howdy!" I said, walking toward the were-wolves. They all turned toward me.

"Who are you?" said Darcourt.

I disguised my voice. I tried to sound like Dusty. "Name's . . . Sandrich."

"Come closer," said Stripe.

I slowly walked forward, keeping my head down.

"How did you know we were here?" asked Darcourt.

"Uh . . . I . . . I was just moseying along, mindin' my own business, and I smelled me some marshmallows."

"I have never seen a wolf your color before," said Stripe. "Is it yellow?"

"Well, now pardner, I prefer to call it *golden*."

"I know all the werewolves around here," said Darcourt. "Never seen you before. Where are you from, Sandrich?"

"Texas," I said.

"Have we met before?" asked Darcourt.

"Nope. Not that I reckon."

"Your scent is highly unusual," said Stripe.

"Yep. Lots of folks tell me that."

What was Martha waiting for?! The wolves were distracted. Why didn't she swoop down and get the book?

"So, uh, maybe I could join your pack?" I said.

"That's a great idea," said Darcourt, reaching into his other saddlebag. He pulled out a wooden box the size of a toaster, with a lot of little, round holes on it. Was that something for the initiation?

He smiled his creepy smile.

"We'd love to have you join our pack . . . Thomas Marks!"

37.

Revealed

He is the Vam-Wolf-Zom!" shouted Stripe. *Finally*, Martha swooped down!

She flew behind Darcourt, toward his motorcycle and the wrapped book. She grabbed the string in her talons. I looked over at her for a second, which I shouldn't have. Darcourt noticed and spun around. He saw her with the book, starting to fly away.

"Thomas! Transform and flee!" she yelled.

Darcourt leaped up into the air. I couldn't

believe how high he jumped. He snatched the book and landed back on the ground. But Martha hung on to it and wouldn't let go. She tugged as hard as she could and tried to fly away, but Darcourt held on tight.

"Thomas! Help!"

As I moved toward Darcourt, he reached into his pocket and pulled out a small silver bottle. He pressed the top and a stream of garlic juice shot out, soaking Martha. She fell to the ground and didn't move.

"Thomas," gasped Martha. "Save yourself. . . . Flee."

I turned into a bat and started to fly away.

But I couldn't desert Martha again. I turned and flew back.

"Thomas . . . don't be a fool!" she said.

Darcourt sprayed me with garlic juice and I fell right next to Martha. It was like getting hit by a baseball bat. I tried to transform to smoke or back to a wolf, but I couldn't. Neither of us could use our powers. We were helpless.

The other werewolves gathered to look down at us.

"So that's a Vam-Wolf-Zom," said Gray Paws.

"Doesn't look like much to me," said Gold Eyes.

Darcourt crouched down and held up the bottle.

"Didn't like my garlic spray, did you? Wards off mosquitos, but it works on vampires too. The wise werewolf always carries one. Now, I need to put you two in a safe place."

Darcourt scooped us up, put us in his wooden box, and closed the lid. I looked out through the tiny holes and saw him pull a Tupperware container out of his saddlebag. He opened it and took out the biggest garlic bulb I had ever seen. It was the size of a softball.

"Elephant garlic," he said, grinning. "Big and powerful."

He set our box down on a rock and carefully placed the garlic bulb on top.

"What are we going to do with those two?" said Stripe.

"They're not going anywhere," said Darcourt. "We'll take the book to the Society of Shape-Shifters. Then, we'll come back and deal with these two."

"Why don't we take the Vam-Wolf-Zom to the Society?" said Gold Eyes.

"One treasure at a time," said Darcourt. "I have bigger plans for him."

And that's when we heard the noise.

38.

Pitter Patter

It sounded like feet tramping through the woods. Through the holes, I saw the werewolves' ears perk up.

"What is that?" said Stripe.

Darcourt peered off into the trees. I heard little kid's voices singing.

"We like, like, like! To hike, hike, hike!"

"It's a large group of children in uniforms, and two adults," said Darcourt. "We must leave!"

I love you, Boy Rangers.

Darcourt turned to Gray Paws and said, "Put the box inside that tree. The trail doesn't come down

here, but we can't risk those kids seeing these two. Douse the fire."

Gray Paws put the garlic torture box, with us inside, in the hollow of a tree trunk. Gold Eyes poured water on the fire and it went out.

"Everyone take different routes in case Martha told other vampires about us," said Darcourt to the others. The werewolves jumped onto their motorcycles and sped off into the night. The Boy Rangers' voices got fainter as they marched away from us.

◦ ◦ ◦

Imagine the worst flu you ever had, and then multiply that a hundred times. That's what it felt like to be near that elephant garlic.

"Will the garlic . . . kill us?" I asked Martha, weakly.

"Garlic cannot . . . kill a vampire. . . . But it can incapacitate it . . . for as long as it remains nearby."

"So, we're going to be here . . . like this . . . forever?"

She nodded. "Unless we are rescued. . . ."

I started to wonder what they would do at the play. Who would do my part? Would they ask Jared to come back?

"There is another problem," said Martha.

"What . . . ?"

"We will eventually need blood. . . . If we do not get any . . . we shall wither away . . . and *succumb*."

I wish I read more books, like Annie. I'd know what *succumb* meant. It didn't sound like a good word.

"What does . . . succumb mean?"

"It means . . . die."

Then we heard something coming toward us. But it wasn't Boy Rangers.

It was a skunk.

39.

Skunked

My dog, Muffin, got sprayed by a skunk once when we were camping. We had to wash him five times before we got the skunk stink out.

"I . . . hate . . . skunks," I said.

"This one . . . you may love," said Martha.

"Why?"

"Watch . . ."

The skunk walked toward us. It stopped about twenty feet away and sniffed. I got a bad feeling in my stomach.

"Do skunks eat bats?" I asked.

"Skunks are omnivores. . . . They prefer small

prey and insects . . . beetles, grasshoppers, mice, rats, moles . . ."

"What about bats?"

"Will you . . . let me finish!"

"Sorry."

"If they are very hungry . . . they eat *plants*."

"Is garlic a plant?"

"Yes, you ninny . . . if he eats it, we are saved."

"Eat it!" I said.

"Shhh!" said Martha. "You'll scare it away."

The skunk came right up to the box and sniffed the garlic bulb.

I quietly said, "Pick it up . . . take it home to your family . . . and eat it . . ."

"Does this skunk speak English?" said Martha.

"Uh . . . no."

"Then be silent."

It picked up the bulb in its claws and put the stem in its mouth. We were saved.

"Yes!" I shouted, which was a big mistake. The skunk got scared and sprayed us.

PEE-EW!

Worst. Smell. Ever. Multiplied a thousand times by my werewolf sense of smell.

But as soon as the skunk walked away with the garlic bulb, we started to feel better and were able to get out of the box.

Martha said, "Now we must find Darcourt . . . and get the book back!"

I was hoping she'd have given up on the whole book thing and I could fly back to school to do the play. I think she could tell I was hoping for that.

"You are not thinking about deserting me *again* are you, Thomas Marks?"

"Me? No!"

40.

Smelly

I picked up Darcourt's scent and we flew over the highway for about fifteen minutes until we saw him below us on his motorcycle.

Martha flew close to me. "See if you can get the book without Darcourt noticing."

"What? *Now*?"

"We cannot wait until he gets to the Society of Shape-Shifters. We will be greatly outnumbered and I am sure they will have garlic at hand."

"How do I get it from him on a moving motorcycle? That's impossible!"

"Think again. His motorcycle is noisy. He is

driving, focusing on the road ahead. And he thinks we are trapped in a box in the woods."

"But he'll smell my scent. The perfume *or* my real scent—he'll know it's me."

"Think *again*: we both stink of skunk. The smell is powerful. If we are lucky, he may think he is passing a skunk that has been run over on the highway."

"I don't know . . ."

"We must try!"

I flew down behind Darcourt's motorcycle, hoping he wouldn't smell me. I held my breath and landed on the saddlebag. It was really noisy that close to the engine.

Darcourt sniffed. "Aw, nasty! That skunk road-kill stinks!"

I carefully climbed up the leather bag. Using my mouth, I undid the strap. It wasn't easy. Try unbuckling a belt with your teeth sometime. I went inside and grabbed the book by the string with my talons. Then I flew straight up and out of the bag. As I turned around and looked back, Darcourt kept going down the highway. He hadn't noticed.

"Well done, Thomas!" Martha said. "He will think the saddlebag came undone and the book fell out."

"Now what?" I said.

"I believe that you have a play to put on. I will make arrangements for the book when we get to your school. First, we must rid ourselves of the skunk scent."

We found a nearby river in the woods and put the book safely on a rock. Martha and I dove in to wash off the skunk smell, and then shook ourselves dry.

It felt like things were going to work out. But the night wasn't over. Sometimes it seems like you solve one problem and then there's a brand-new problem to deal with. Tonight there would be more than one problem.

41.

A Backstage Visitor

We landed in the shadows behind the auditorium. It was seven thirty. I was half an hour late. Lubick would not be happy.

"Bat to human, human I shall be!"

We both turned human. Well, Martha did. I turned back to a werewolf.

"I'd better get ready for the play," I said.

"I am indebted to you for your help in retrieving the book. I shall not forget it. And for coming back for me. 'Twas foolish, but a brave and noble act."

She gave me a hug. It lasted three seconds. I've started to count how long hugs are. I don't know why. When the hug ended, she kept her hands on my shoulders.

"Thank you, Tom."

I don't think she'd ever called me Tom before.

She had also never kissed me. Which is what she did next. Her lips were cold, but it didn't bother me. I had now been kissed by four girls in one week. I bet that was a record for a twelve-year old. Definitely for this Vam-Wolf-Zom.

Martha said, "I must leave now and get the book to a safe place."

"Oh . . . you're not going to stay to see the play?"

"You wish me to?"

"Well, uh, I mean, you don't have to."

She smiled. "I do enjoy the theater. And Darcourt will not notice the book is gone for a good spell. And he would certainly not come here looking for it."

"Thomas Marks, where have you been?!"

It was Ms. Lubick coming towards us. Martha ducked into the shadows. Lubick was holding a large ax with a shiny blade. It looked like she wanted to cut my head off, but luckily it was a prop ax for the play. "Your call time was seven o'clock! What happened?"

"Sorry, Ms. Lubick. I . . . I . . . ran into a gang." That was sort of the truth.

"A gang?" she said.

"Yeah, there were four of them, but I got away and—"

She looked at me more closely. "What on earth have you done to your fur?"

I'd forgotten about that.

"Oh . . . yeah . . . uh . . . I dyed it. That's why I'm late. I think Sandrich would be a blond monster."

"I think you mean yellow. Well, we'll just have to live with it. I have some emergency food offstage in case you get hungry. Get in costume and start vocal warm-ups!"

Lubick ran back into the auditorium.

Martha stepped back into the light. "Break a leg, Thomas."

o o o

I passed Zeke on the way to the dressing room. He was in his silver-and-red robot costume, carrying his laser sword.

"T-Man, I knew you'd make it! I kept telling everybody, don't worry, Tom'll be here."

"Thanks, Zeke. I'll tell you what happened later! I gotta get ready!"

"Your fur looks cool!" he said, and ran off. He'd probably be the only person who liked it.

Nobody was in the dressing room, since the cast was already in their costumes. As I started putting on my costume, I heard a voice behind me.

"Are you the kid playing the monster?"

I turned around. It was a tall guy, with dark hair and big muscles everywhere you could have a muscle. He had to duck coming in the doorway.

He was either a high school football player, or a superhero I hadn't heard about.

"Yeah. I am," I said as I pulled on a boot.

"Nice makeup," he said

"Actually, I'm not wearing makeup. This is how I look when there's a full moon." I pulled on my other boot. "I gotta get ready 'cause the play's about to start."

"I'm Bernardo. Bella's boyfriend."

My stomach did a flip-flop.

"Oh . . . I . . . I think she's onstage or in the girl's dressing room next door."

"I don't want to see her. I want to see you."

"Why . . . ?"

"Just wanted to tell you that if you kiss her tonight, you're dead."

Why had this stupid kiss turned into such a big thing with everybody?!

"It's just a pretend kiss!" I said. "We're acting!" He didn't look like he believed me. "Actually, I—I don't even like kissing her."

"Why not?! What's the matter with her?"

"Nothing! I mean, it's not bad kissing her. It's nice, but it's not that nice!" I had to shut up.

"If your lips touch her lips, I'm gonna kill you."

Didn't he know that Vam-Wolf-Zoms are really hard to kill?

I was going to tell him that Bella and I had already kissed six times during rehearsal, but I decided he might try to kill me right there.

He said, "Take my advice. No kiss."

He walked out.

I hate theater.

42.

A Surprise Visitor

Hey, Mr. Actor Dude!"
Carrot Boy was standing in the door,
wearing a backpack.

"Oh— Hi— I gotta get ready," I said, pulling on
my jacket. "The play starts in five minutes!"

"I know. I just wanted you to see who I brought
to the show."

A man poked his head around the corner. He
was wearing a dark suit and gloves, a hat pulled
down low over his face, sunglasses, and had a big,
long beard.

"I reckon I couldn't miss this here show," he said. The man took off the sunglasses and pulled down what turned out to be a fake beard.

I couldn't believe it. "Dusty! What— How'd you—"

"I called Lucas to see if he'd come fetch me, and he kindly said, 'Totally dude!' So here I am."

Carrot Boy started to open the backpack he had brought. "This is stuffed with hot dogs, chicken nuggets, and beef jerky, so he won't get hungry."

"And he brought along this here disguise, so nobody'd get in a tither about a zombie in the theater," said Dusty.

"Thanks, Lucas," I said. It was always weird to call him Lucas.

"You'd better get yourself onstage," said Dusty. "You got a show to do. Knock 'em dead!"

43.

The Play Goes On and On and On

I went onstage. I could hear the audience on the other side of the curtain, taking their seats and talking. I peeked out through a hole in the curtain and saw Bernardo sitting in the front row near Mom, Dad, and Emma. Carrot Boy was sitting with Dusty on the aisle. Way in the back, I saw Martha Livingston reading the program.

"Glad you could make it," said Annie, who came up behind me. "Why are you yellow?"

"I was so worried about you," said Capri.

Abel looked me over. "You resemble *Canis*

lupaster, the African wolf, known for its golden coat."

"You look like Big Bird," said Dog Hots.

I saw Tanner and could tell he wanted to say something, but he didn't.

Lubick got the cast to form a circle and stood in the middle.

"People, I am extremely proud of you. I know it hasn't been easy getting to this night. Remember, this is live theater, so there are bound to be some surprises. If something goes wrong, do what you can to fix it and keep going. We don't want Dionysus, the god of theater, coming down from Mount Olympus and cursing us, do we? On with the show!"

We took our places for the first scene. Bella came up to me. She was in her space princess costume and looked pretty amazing.

"Tom, I have to tell you something," she said. Her voice sounded different. It was lower.

"What?"

"You know how I feel about you, right?"

"Uh . . . yeah." She'd been really nice to me all week, but I didn't know what she meant.

"Tom. I think I'm . . ."

Had Bella fallen in love with me? An eighth

grader in love with a sixth grader? Who was also a Vam-Wolf-Zom? Did her giant, crazy boyfriend know about this?

"... I'm coming down with a bad cold."

"Oh . . ."

I guess she wasn't in love with me.

"I don't want to give it to you. So, you don't have to kiss me. Unless you want to. Or we can do a fake kiss. You know, cup our hands and put them up by our mouths and pretend to kiss behind them. It's up to you."

I quickly made two lists in my mind.

IF I KISS BELLA

1. I might get a cold
2. Lubick will be happy
3. Bernardo will kill me

IF I DON'T KISS BELLA

1. I won't get a cold
2. Lubick will kill me
3. Bernardo won't kill me
4. That Dionysus guy will come down from Mount Olympus and curse me

"Okay," I said to Bella. "Can I decide later?"

She nodded and sneezed.

"Curtain goes up in ten seconds!" said Lubick.

Zeke gave me a thumbs-up. Annie gave me a fist bump and said, "Have a good show." Capri hugged me. It lasted four seconds.

○ ○ ○

The show began. The audience laughed at the funny parts and were quiet during the serious parts. They clapped a lot after every song. I knew they would, since everybody in the audience knew somebody onstage. Capri kept trying to push her way to the front of the stage in the villager scenes. Zeke dropped his laser sword.

Bella sang her first song, "Don't Call Me Princess, That Isn't My Name" better than Carolyn ever did, even though her nose was stuffed up.

I did my first song, "It's Not Easy Being a Monster." I messed up one line, but I don't think people noticed.

Annie, as Tara the thief, did her song, "Stealin' for a Livin'," and the audience went crazy. I bet that next year she gets the lead part.

It was fun doing the show. I didn't want it to end. But then, all of a sudden, it was time for the last scene. I still hadn't decided whether or not to kiss Bella.

"Sandrich . . . I want to kiss you," she said.

She put her hands up to the sides of my face for the fake kiss. I didn't do anything. I saw Zeke, offstage, over Bella's shoulder. I could tell from his face that he thought I'd forgotten what I was supposed to do. He puckered up his lips and pointed at them.

I half expected Emma to shout out from the audience, "You quack me up!" I bet she wanted to. I also bet Dad was giving her dirty looks. Bernardo was probably getting ready to leap onstage and murder me.

I whispered to Bella, "I don't care if I get a cold."

I pulled her hands down from my face. She smiled. I leaned in. She leaned in. Our lips were about one inch from each other. And that's when I saw Martha Livingston coming down the side aisle toward the stage. The audience was dark, but I could see her with my night vision. What was she doing?! She pointed behind her. I couldn't believe what I saw, slowly coming down the aisle.

It was Darcourt.

44.

The Other Surprise Visitors

Somehow, Darcourt had figured out we had the book and where we were.

How'd he find us? Our scents? A wild guess? It didn't matter. Darcourt had almost caught up with Martha and was reaching out to grab her. She threw the book to me onstage, just as somebody on the aisle stuck their leg out and tripped Darcourt. He stumbled and fell facedown on the floor as Martha went up the stairs and onto the side of the stage.

Darcourt stood up, looking mad. I heard Dusty whisper, "Sorry, pardner. Had to stretch my leg."

Darcourt stormed out the side door. Where was he going?

Meanwhile, onstage, Bella was giving me a What-Are-You-Doing? look.

I said, "Before we kiss, Princess Felice . . . I must do something."

Martha was offstage in the wings. I saw Lubick next to her, freaking out. Martha looked her in the eyes and started hypnotizing her. Lubick's head slowly nodded. Martha is amazingly fast at hypnotizing since she's been doing it for over two hundred years.

"Oh . . . look!" I said, holding up the book. "A book has magically appeared! I wonder what it is?"

Bella gave me another crazy look.

Lubick, whose eyes were half closed, whispered to Bella from off-stage, "This is a new scene I forgot to tell you about. . . . Follow Tom's lead."

I held up the book. "This is . . . uh . . . the long, lost book of spells . . . with the cure for my curse! It will turn me back into a prince!"

By now the rest of the cast and crew were standing in the wings watching us, wondering what was going on.

Then, I heard a creaking noise above me. I looked up and saw Darcourt on the wooden walkway above the stage. He was no longer human—he

was full-on wolf. What was he going to do? More importantly, what was I going to do? I saw Zeke offstage and got an idea.

"Send me Robot Number Three!" I shouted. "I must speak to him!"

Zeke ran onstage and bowed down on one knee.

"I am here, m'lord! What do you wish?"

I bent down and whispered, "Tell Dog Hots to turn on the strobe light." Then, I stood up straight and said out loud, "I just wanted to thank you for protecting the princess."

"It is an honor to serve the princess! It is my sacred duty! It is—"

"Go!"

Zeke ran off and grabbed Dog Hots, who turned on the strobe light. It flashed and made everything look black and white and jerky. I hoped it would hide whatever was going to happen next.

Darcourt jumped down onto the stage and landed on all fours in front of me. The audience went crazy and I could hear them talking.

"How many kids are inside that costume?"

"That's not a costume, it's a dog!"

"Looks like a wolf to me!"

"They're not going to have a wolf onstage!"

"They have a Vam-Wolf-Zom onstage!"

"Quiet! I'm trying to enjoy the play!"

"Oh no!" I said. "It is the evil Demon Dog from the Planet Darcourt, who I forgot to tell you about earlier! I must not let it get the magic book! Princess Felice, go hide!"

Bella ran offstage.

Darcourt and I slowly circled each other.

"Give me the book and this ends without blood," he whispered.

"No way," I said.

"Then we must fight."

"Bring it on."

He jumped on me and we both fell to the floor. We must have looked like dogs play-wrestling. But we were definitely not playing. The audience loved it. They probably thought we had a really well-trained dog.

I was going to throw the book back to Martha offstage, so she could transform and fly away. But Darcourt clamped his fangs down on the book and yanked it out of my hands. He started to run offstage. I ran after him and jumped on his back. I flipped him over and pried open his jaw. I got the book back and started running toward the other side of the stage. The audience cheered.

The book was gross and slobbery and it slipped out of my hands, landing on the floor in the center of the stage. Zeke ran onstage to grab it while Darcourt and I both raced toward it.

Zeke grabbed the book and shouted, "I got it, T-Man—I mean Sandrich!"

Darcourt lowered his head and charged at Zeke. He lifted Zeke up in the air with his snout, and Zeke went flying. His laser sword hit a spotlight, knocking it down. It looked like the one Dog Hots had hung.

The spotlight fell toward Zeke and the book. I had to catch Zeke first. Darcourt went for the book, but before he got there the spotlight landed on top of it. Sparks flew and the book burst into flames for a second. Then, there was only smoke.

When the smoke cleared, the book was just a pile of ashes. Martha was going to kill me. Darcourt looked down at it, then up at me. He growled and ran offstage and out the side door.

The audience applauded and cheered.

I decided I'd better end the play. I looked toward Bella in the wings and reached out my hand.

"Come back, Princess Felice! It is safe now. I promise."

Bella cautiously walked back onstage. I took her hand.

"Alas, the book of spells has been destroyed, so I shall remain a monster forever."

I whispered to her, "Say 'I don't care.'"

She did.

Then. Finally. I kissed her. A real one.

I nodded to Tanner, who was in the wings, and he pulled the curtain down.

"Bows!" said Lubick.

The very confused cast ran onstage for our bows. The curtain went up and the audience jumped to their feet and clapped and cheered and whistled.

Carrot Boy shouted out, "Bring on the dog!"

Everybody looked around, but of course "the dog" did not come back to take a bow. Bella took a solo bow, and I did too. Then, we took a bow together and she kissed me . . . *again*. I looked down at Bernardo in the front row. He didn't look like the happiest person in the world. I decided to worry about him later.

When the curtain came down again, Lubick joined us onstage.

"Fabulous show!" said Lubick. "I hope you all liked my little surprise!"

Martha Livingston was definitely the greatest hypnotist in the world. I looked over to find her, and saw her slipping out the side door.

45.

Questions and Answers

I needed to get away from everyone asking me a million questions about what had just happened. I used the excuse that always works: "I gotta go to the bathroom!" and went outside to find Martha. Was she going to get the Vampire Death Squad and have them kill me because the book got destroyed?

She was sitting in the shadows on a bench behind the auditorium.

"Martha . . . I'm sorry about the book."

She let out a long sigh. "So am I. . . . But better

the book was destroyed than back in Darcourt's hands."

I couldn't believe she said that. "Really?"

"There are still a few other copies. And with Lovick Zabrecky, who gave it to me, long gone, I need not fear his wrath." She smiled. "And truthfully? It is somewhat a relief to no longer worry about it."

Now that I knew she wasn't going to kill me, I sat down next to her.

"When did Darcourt get here?" I said.

"During the final scene. I sensed his presence behind me. I knew he would not attack me in the theater, so I decided to get the book to you. I had no idea he would go onstage. However, it did make for a thrilling end to the play."

"Yeah. But I wished we'd done the quiet, normal ending."

"The Society of Shape-Shifters will not be pleased with Darcourt, and they are not a group one wants to disappoint. I do not think we shall see him for a long time."

"Good!"

"Tom, I have a question I'd like to ask you."

She reached out and held my hand. Her hand was cold, but really soft. She looked at me with her green eyes.

"That was insane!" said Annie, who was walking toward us with Capri. "Whose dog was that?"

I let go of Martha's hand and tried to think up something. "Uh . . ."

"'Twas mine," said Martha. "I am friends with your drama teacher, who asked to borrow him for the performance as a special surprise."

"Seriously?" said Annie, who sounded like she didn't believe it.

"Hey, you're the girl we met on Halloween," said Capri. "The one that talks weird."

"Good evening, Capri," said Martha. "Your performance as Townsperson Number Seven was . . . unforgettable."

"Why are you still dressed as a vampire?" asked Annie.

"Yeah," said Capri. "Halloween was four months ago."

"I am attending a costume party later," said Martha.

"I thought you were moving to New Orleans," said Annie.

"Your memory is excellent, Annie. As was your performance." Martha smiled, but not so you could see her fangs. "Thomas was also outstanding, don't you think?"

"Yeah," said Capri, turning to me. "Why'd Bella kiss you twice?"

I shrugged. It's really the best answer for almost any question.

Annie said, "Lubick says we have to get out of our costumes now because they want to lock up the auditorium. See you at the cast party?"

I had forgotten about that. "Yeah. Definitely."

Capri had a serious look on her face. "Are you coming to the party, Martha?"

"No. I am afraid I must depart," said Martha, standing up.

"Too bad," said Capri with a big smile. She and Annie walked off, whispering to each other. I could have listened, but I had an important question to ask Martha.

"Where are you going?"

"That was awesome, Tom!" said Carrot Boy, walking up with Dusty.

"That's what I call one heck of a show," said Dusty. "Reminded me of my rodeo days, rasslin' steers."

"You must be Dusty," said Martha.

"And you must be Martha Livingston."

Carrot Boy leaned in. "And I must be Lucas!"

Martha smiled and stared intently at Carrot Boy. "Hello, Lucas . . . Why don't you go sit over at the table for a while?"

She'd hypnotized him even faster than she did Zeke on Halloween.

"I'll . . . go . . . over . . . there," said Carrot Boy, walking away.

"Mighty pleased to make your acquaintance, Miss Martha," said Dusty. "Tom speaks quite highly of you."

"Does he now?" she said.

"I saw you trip Darcourt, Dusty," I said. "How'd you know it was him?"

"I noticed Miss Martha sittin' in the back. Figured out pretty quick who she was. Then, I saw that tall feller come down the aisle after her and figured he was Darcourt. So, I reckoned I'd better do somethin'. Zombies can't do much, but I decided to slow him down a bit."

"And you sure did!" said a voice I was surprised to hear.

It was Darcourt.

He was in human form, walking towards us. Martha and I both tensed up.

"Relax," he said, smiling. "I come in peace. We've got nothing to fight about anymore. The book is toast. Well, actually it's *ashes*."

"Better 'tis ash, than whole, and in your hands," said Martha.

"You always had a way with words, Martha." He turned to Dusty and held out his hand. "I'm Darcourt."

"Name's Dusty. But I don't much like to shake hands with people who treat my friends badly."

Darcourt sniffed. "I smell . . . zombie."

"And I smell me a low-down, dirty varmint," said Dusty.

I looked at Martha, Dusty, and Darcourt. For the first time I was with the three people who made me what I am today . . . a Vam-Wolf-Zom.

"Okay, I gotta know something," said Darcourt. "How'd you two escape from the box?"

"A skunk came along and ate the garlic," I said.

"*That's* why I smelled skunk when I was driving! It was you getting the book. Smooth move, Tom."

"Why are you still here, Darcourt?" said Martha. "I should think you would be running away with great haste. The Society of Shape-Shifters will be looking for you."

He glanced over his shoulder, then back at us. "I appreciate your concern, Martha. I just want to know one more thing: How you knew *where* and *when* my pack was meeting. Who's the informant? Gray Paws? Gold Eyes? Stripe?"

Martha stared at him. "I haven't the slightest idea what you are talking about."

"Mister L! What are you doing out here?"

Emma had come outside and looked annoyed with Carrot Boy, who was still sitting at the table, staring off into space. Martha snapped her fingers. He blinked and stood up.

"Waiting for you, Ms. E."

Emma came over to us. "How cool was it that Dusty showed up? That was my idea."

"It was Dusty's idea," said Carrot Boy.

Emma ignored him. "You were pretty good, Tom, but you should've let me teach you some of my acting secrets—Oh my God! Darcourt! I don't believe it! It's me, Emma! Remember? We met at Comic-Con?"

"How could I *ever* forget you?" said Darcourt.

"And I'm Lucas. Remember? Her *boyfriend.*"

"You're one lucky dude," said Darcourt. "Well, I gotta make tracks. Martha, always a pleasure. Dusty, nice to meet you. Tom, I bet our paths will cross again."

"You have to go right now?" said Emma, who looked like she'd just been told she couldn't go shopping for a year.

"Yeah, I'm going on a long vacation to parts unknown. Later!"

He walked off toward his motorcycle in the parking lot.

"I am Martha Livingston. You must be Emma?"

Emma turned to Martha. "Yeah—cute dress! Wait . . . Martha Livingston? You wrote that note to Tom. You're one of his girlfriends."

"Emma!" I said.

"I am a girl. I am a friend," said Martha. "I am fond of your brother. But there has been no declaration of affection."

I wanted to turn to smoke and disappear.

Dusty turned to Carrot Boy. "Lucas, we've got

ourselves a long drive back to Zombie Nirvana. We'd better hit the trail."

"Thanks for coming, Dusty," I said. "I really appreciate it."

"Wouldn't've missed it for the world. Emma, Miss Martha, it was pleasure." He tipped his hat.

Martha curtseyed.

"See you tomorrow, Em," said Carrot Boy.

"No way! I'm coming with you and Dusty," said Emma. "We can sing songs all the way to Zombie Nirvana!"

Dusty gulped. "That will surely make the trip a memorable one."

I felt sorry for Dusty as they walked off.

"I think I shall follow Darcourt," said Martha.

"Why?"

"Never trust a werewolf."

"You can trust me."

She smiled. "Yes. I believe I can."

"So . . . are you coming back sometime?"

"You may count on it, Thomas Marks."

She changed into a bat. I stood there and watched her fly away, until she was just a black speck.

46.

Endings and Beginnings

The cast party was at a restaurant nearby. Everybody kept talking about the dog and asking questions. Lubick told them she and I had worked it out as a surprise. I just nodded my head. Annie talked to Tanner practically the whole party. Capri kept asking me about Martha. Bella showed up with Bernardo, who gave me dirty looks, but he didn't try to kill me. Zeke had asked Lubick if he could keep his laser sword and she said yes. So he had it tucked into his belt. Dog Hots kept saying, "I tightened that spotlight, I know I tightened it!" to anybody who'd listen to him.

I was heading to the bathroom when Tanner walked up.

"Did Lubick and you really plan that thing with the dog?" he asked.

"Yeah," I lied.

"It looked like a wolf to me."

I played dumb. "It's a Siberian husky. I guess they look like wolves."

"My uncle raises Siberian huskies. They don't get that big."

I shrugged. He leaned forward. I automatically backed up. It was a natural reaction after years of being afraid of him.

"I promise I won't tell anybody," he whispered. "Was that a werewolf?"

"Yeah."

I don't know why I told him. I don't know why I trusted him. But I did.

○ ○ ○

On Monday morning, I was walking to the bus stop. I felt kind of sad that the play was over and we wouldn't get to rehearse anymore. Then, I thought about how cool it was that Lucas brought Dusty to see the show, and the way Martha Livingston had kissed me.

I used to think it was the worst thing in the world to be a Vam-Wolf-Zom. If I had a time machine, I'd go back and change everything so I could be a normal kid. But if I *wasn't* a Vam-Wolf-Zom I wouldn't have met Martha or Dusty. And I wouldn't have a great voice for the band, and I wouldn't have been in the play, and Tanner Gantt would still be a bully. I guess what I mean is there's a lot of bad stuff about being a Vam-Wolf-Zom, but there's some good stuff too.

"T-Man!"

Zeke was running down the sidewalk. He stopped and put his hands on his knees to catch his breath.

"What happened, Zeke?"

"The most awesome . . . amazing . . . crazy . . . excellent thing . . . ever!"

Zeke says stuff like that a lot. It could be that he heard they were making a new Vacuum Girl movie. Or there was going to be a Rabbit Attacks! TV show. Or he just saw a cat whose eyes were different colors.

"Tell me," I said.

He took a deep breath. "I was watching the news . . . when I was having my breakfast . . . cranberry crunch cereal . . . and orange juice and toast . . ."

"Okay, okay!" I said impatiently. "What is it?"

He looked up.

"There's a girl in London. . . . Her name is Constance Brookledge. . . ."

"So?"

"She's a Vam-Wolf-Zom."

Acknowledgments

Does anyone really read the acknowledgement page?

You do, because you are cool.

I want to thank the following:

Don Chadwick and Bill Stumpf for designing the Aeron chair, where I spend a lot of time sitting and writing. My back thanks you too.

Arnold Schwarzenegger and Shaquille O'Neal, who helped me to be able to write this book. Drop by my house and I'll explain why.

Larry McMurtry, author of *Lonesome Dove*, who inspired me to make the zombie a cowboy.

Mark Fearing, for all his terrific illustrations.

Jud Laghi, my agent, who does the business stuff so I can concentrate on the writing stuff.

William Gibson, who wrote a play called *Dinny & The Witches* that I did in high school. I played Dinny and got to kiss four girls. I love theater.

George Sheanshang, my lawyer, who reads the fine print.

Annette Banks for reading the drafts and for her helpful notes.

Sara DiSalvo, Michelle Montague, Alison Tarnofsky, and the rest of the team at Holiday House who get these books out into the world, and to YOU, the cool person still reading this page.

My friends Doug, Tommy, Elliot, Mike, Penn, Peter, John #1, John #2, John #3, Rich, Gary, Gene, Bob, and the others who will get mad when they don't see their names here. These books are about friendship (I hope you noticed), and I am lucky to have an assortment of unique and special people I am grateful to call "friends."

Lauren Forte, the eagle-eyed copy editor who finds my mistakes and fixes them.

Living and dead writers who inspire me: John Steinbeck (who wrote my favorite book, *Cannery*

Row—I have a signed first edition, and I'll show it to you when you come to my house to ask about Arnold and Shaq), Annie Baker, Maryrose Wood, P.G. Wodehouse, Simon Rich, Kurt Vonnegut, S.J. Perlman, J.K. Rowling, Roald Dahl, Stephen Sondheim, and Ian Fleming.

Bob Baker, my high school drama teacher, who was nothing like the drama teacher in this book. He changed my life and taught me about the value of hard work, taking your profession seriously, and how to have a lifelong passion for the arts.

Write your name here: _____. (You read this page and deserve to be acknowledged.)